"Who is it?" Lanie called guardedly

"It's me — Jard!" She caught the note of suppressed anger in his voice. "And you'd better let me in. I've got things to say to you." For a moment she hesitated, then she opened the door. He towered above her, dominant, erect and menacing. It was clear that he meant business.

"Now look here," she said defiantly, "If you're on again about my taking on the job with you and your dad...." His thick dark eyebrows rose sardonically. "How did you guess?"

She ignored his sarcasm. "It wasn't my idea!"

He pinned her with his hard accusing gaze. "Are you telling me I can't believe the evidence of my eyes?"

"I don't care what you believe." Frustration welled up inside her. She couldn't let this strange angry man misunderstand her any longer!

The Rouseabout Girl

Gloria Bevan

Harlequin Books

TORONTO • NEW YORK • LONDON
AMSTERDAM • PARIS • SYDNEY • HAMBURG
STOCKHOLM • ATHENS • TOKYO • MILAN

Original hardcover edition published in 1983
by Mills & Boon Limited

ISBN 0-373-02563-7

Harlequin Romance first edition August 1983

CHAPTER ONE

EVEN before she reached the entrance leading to the spacious reception area Lanie caught the loud buzz of conversation and laughter echoing from the lavishly decorated room. At the open doorway she stood hesitating, then realised that an impeccably attired young man with dark-rimmed glasses and a welcoming smile was hurrying towards her. 'Tell me, you're not— you don't happen to be our prizewinner in our flour promotion contest?'

She smiled up at him. 'That's me! Lanie Petersen.'

His eyes crinkled in a look of amusement. 'We weren't expecting anyone quite so young!'

Lanie wrinkled her nose at him. 'I'm nineteen!' she said with spirit, but he merely grinned. She could almost read his thoughts. 'It's ridiculous that she could be our prizewinner. Why, she looks little more than a schoolgirl!' It was a reactionary thing and she had come to expect it, something to do with being only an inch or so over five feet with a dimpled round face into the bargain. It was annoying not to look her age, but over the years she had become accustomed to it.

'John Garfield!' He shot out a hand and took her small paw in a strong grip. 'General manager of the outfit. May I offer my congratulations on your winning entry? The general opinion of the company was that your recipe was outstanding and the advertising agency who judged the contest assured us they had no hesitation whatever in awarding you the prize.'

'Thank you.' As he bent to pin her name-tag to the shoulder of her dress Lanie couldn't help giggling to herself. Imagine me, at a shareholder's meeting, she thought. A quick glance around the crowded room and she estimated there was scarcely a man or woman here under the age of fifty. Golly, she thought, I must be the

5

only girl in the whole place. A dimple flickered at each corner of her soft lips. I'm a shareholder in the company—or I soon will be. I can't believe it!

'This way, please,' her escort was saying, and she went with him over the deep-piled carpet as they threaded their way between the festively decorated tables. There was a lightness in her step and her face was upturned to the man at her side. She was barely aware of appreciative masculine glances and envious feminine looks as watchers followed the progress of the slim young figure, flower-fresh in a simple white sun-frock, a cloud of bright hair that just missed being red falling over the shoe-string ties on lightly-tanned shoulders.

'Unfortunately,' her companion said, 'there doesn't seem to be a vacant table. We had one specially reserved for you among the V.I.Ps,' his eyes twinkled behind thick lensed glasses, 'but someone has beaten you to it. Shall I ask him to move away?'

'Oh no,' she protested in her soft husky tones, 'it doesn't matter a bit. Couldn't we share it?'

'If you're quite sure.'

At last they reached a table occupied by a spare elderly man with carefully brushed white hair. Lanie smiled down into the lined, sun-weathered face. 'Do you mind if I share your table?'

'Delighted.' With old-fashioned courtesy he rose to his feet and saw her seated. The manager made a brief introduction. 'Jim Sanderson. Jim happens to be one of our main shareholders in the firm.'

The leathery face split into a grin. 'Only because I happen to grow wheat for your mill!' He had shrewd bright eyes, Lanie noticed, and he was so deeply tanned. Face, arms and neck were all a shade of mahogany. Clearly he was a *tanata whenua*—the Maori words sprang to her mind, a man of the land. Could that be the reason she got the impression he was feeling hot and uncomfortable this warm summer day in his city gear of well-cut grey suit and crisp white shirt?

She brought her mind back to the pleasant masculine

tones. 'Seems like you and I are the only ones who are here on our own.'

She sent him a twinkling glance.

'Does it matter?'

'Not now.' His glance went to her name-tag. 'It's Elaine, is it?'

'Goodness, no!' She flashed him a smile. 'No one ever calls me that. Just Lanie.'

'Just Lanie.' His glance flickered over her short nose with its scattering of freckles, the wide happy smile. There was something about this girl's air of vitality and friendliness that made him feel young again. Suddenly he got the feeling that the deadly boring annual meeting of shareholders had been worth getting himself togged up for in this flaming hot suit and tie, after all. This girl was happy-natured, an enthusiast, like his own girl. A shadow clouded his eyes. Funny to think that though his only daughter had married in England and lived there for the past fifteen years, he still missed her around the place. She was the sort of girl who made life seem fresh and exciting, and he wouldn't mind betting that this Elaine was the same. Odd that they both happened to have the same name too. Aloud he murmured pleasantly, 'Quite a crowd for the meeting.' His glance roved over the room with its many sun-tanned faces. 'Looks like wheat-growers from all over the country are having a day out in the city. All but you.' He had a really friendly smile, Lanie thought. 'My guess is that you belong right here in town.'

She glanced towards him in surprise. 'What makes you say that?'

He grinned. 'Never came across anyone in the country looking the way you do,' his eyes crinkled, 'worse luck!' Something in his expression robbed the words of any personal significance. Indeed, Lanie felt extraordinarily pleased at the compliment. Of course she knew she looked fairly attractive in a diminutive, flame-coloured-hair, extra-slim sort of way. How could she help knowing? All the same it was heartwarming to be told so, especially today, when she was in need of all the encouragement that came her way.

'Forgive me,' there was a glimmer of curiosity in the twinkling brown eyes, 'but aren't you a trifle young for this sort of caper?'

'I do feel a bit out of it here today,' she admitted. She sent him a wide and friendly smile. She enjoyed talking to people, and her habit of confiding her life story to strangers was one that was bound to land her in some sort of trouble sooner or later, her flatmate Mary often warned her. 'You see, it was this way——' She broke off as a waiter pushed a trolley towards the table. There was a tempting array of foods, both sweet and savoury, together with pots of tea and coffee. 'Shall I be mother?'

'If you please. Coffee for me. I'll tell you something else,' her companion observed when they had helped themselves to cold meats and attractively presented salads, 'I don't see you as a shareholder in the firm. Like I said, you're at least twenty years too young. Tell me, what *are* you doing here amongst all the old fogies like me?'

Two dimples flickered at the corners of Lanie's soft lips. Her mischievous smile, her companion mused, was something worth watching for. His own Elaine had smiled like that, as if she really meant it, as if life was worth living, every damned moment of it!

'Would you believe,' Lanie buttered a roll, 'I've got a special invitation to the luncheon today! I'm hard up at the moment,' she confided, 'and a free meal isn't to be turned down, not when you're down to your last few dollars and out of a job!'

If her companion was surprised he hid it well. 'Shares,' he agreed, 'are good to own, but you can't have them for dinner.' There was a kindly twinkle in his brown eyes. 'Let me guess? A well-heeled uncle passed on the luncheon invitation, right?'

She eyed him laughingly. 'Wrong! And I haven't any shares in the company—not yet, that is, but I soon will have!' She leaned forward confidentially. 'Guess what!'

'Your parents are passing on a few hundred or so as a birthday gift to you?'

A shadow passed over her face. 'No parents—they died when I was a child. Luckily I had a nice aunt who brought me up. But my parents didn't have any capital. They had so little to come and go on they didn't leave me a thing.' She grinned impishly. 'Except this red hair.' Flicking a shining red-gold strand with her finger, she pulled a face, then murmured as an afterthought, 'And the bread recipe, of course!'

'Bread recipe?'

'Oh yes, that's the point, that's why I happen to be here today. Don't look so puzzled,' she ran on impulsively, 'it's quite simple really. Just that I happened to see a competition advertised in the local newspaper. It was run by the flour company, and all you had to do was to submit an unusual recipe for home-made bread. I still have my mother's old cookery book, all in her handwriting, and I thought her recipe was a bit unusual.'

He was an attentive listener, studying her with amused interest. 'Must have been a cracker, chockful of modern health foods and all that?'

'Oh no, it was so simple a child could follow it. You just throw three cups of flour in a basin, toss in three teaspoons of baking powder with two tablespoons of sugar and a teaspoon of salt. Then you sift it all together and mix it up with ten fluid ounces of beer. It only takes an hour to bake and there you are! How does it strike you?'

He chuckled. 'The same way it would strike any man—a waste of a good bottle of beer!'

'Oh, but you haven't tasted the loaf. Anyway, the flour milling people sent me a letter asking me to be here today so that they can present me with the prizes.'

'You don't look too happy about it. What is the prize? A sack of flour?'

A bubble of laughter rose to her lips. 'Worse than that! They sent me a picture of it—a massive electric range with all the latest gadgets. Honestly, the way it looks in the photograph you'd need to hold a driving licence to work it!' All at once her expression sobered.

'That's one of the reasons why I decided to give in my notice at the office and look for work somewhere in the country. Making the break now seemed to work in with everything else.'

Everything else? In the silence her thoughts wandered and a picture of Trevor's set, resentful face flashed before her mental vision. He had been so *angry* when she handed back her diamond solitaire engagement ring. Working at adjacent desks in the same office, they had drifted into a tepid relationship that on Lanie's part had been more a matter of habit and companionship than anything else. When Trevor had told her with pride of the amount of his savings and had suggested a marriage date, all at once she had panicked. Was this what life was all about? A gold band on her finger, a boxlike house in the suburbs? What of the wild sweet ecstasy of love? Or could it be that was something that existed only in films and romantic novels?

It was true that the contest win had sparked off her decision to break with the past and to start a new life. She had spent her childhood in a small country town, sliding down grassy banks and riding her pony to school and she still preferred country living to the bustle of city streets. Over the last few years, she had managed to keep up her interest in horse riding and had become a familiar figure at local shows and gymkhanas. There must surely be some sort of work offering in a country settlement, she had thought—but although she had written many letters of application to banks and councils and made numerous phone calls, so far nothing had eventuated for her in the way of employment. If she didn't find something soon she'd be forced to apply for another job in the city to supplement her dwindling resources. She would just have to, she thought desperately.

Her companion's voice jerked her from her musing. 'Burned your boats behind you, is that it?'

She nodded. 'Do you think it was a stupid thing to do?'

'Not a bit of it!' he assured her warmly. 'Give it a go,

if that's what you want.'

'It's just,' she picked at the oyster pattie on her plate, 'that I don't know what I do want. Just some job in the country, I guess, something . . . different.'

'You've done the right thing,' he assured her, and his definite tone made Lanie feel encouraged all over again. 'You'll win out, not a doubt about it. Take a chance in life and you'll be surprised at what can happen!' His voice took on an appreciative note, 'You must be a top-notcher in the kitchen department! Cordon Bleu meals every day of the week, is that the way it is?'

'Goodness, no! It was only a recipe I got the prizes for.' Her face brightened. 'Oh, and there are one hundred shares in the company as well!'

'There you are, then,' he told her triumphantly, 'you are a shareholder here after all, or you will be at any minute. Congratulations!' He pushed a laden plate towards her. 'Have another cream cake on the strength of it.'

'Thank you.' Lanie helped herself to a fluffy butterfly sponge cake oozing rich dairy cream. She had no problem about keeping her weight down, on the contrary, and with this meal she would be able to skip dinner tonight and conserve her dwindling resources.

All at once she realised that the main business of the meeting had begun, as shareholders were made aware of the financial situation of the firm. To Lanie the reports and speeches seemed to go on for ever, and she fell to reviewing her own financial position. Who would have believed that job-chasing, with its outlay in bus fares, postage stamps and toll calls, could run away with so much money?

The sound of her own name jerked her back to the present and she became aware of John Garfield, who was approaching the table. 'It's the presentation of the prizes!' in near panic she appealed to her newly-found friend. 'What on earth will I say?'

He smiled encouragingly. 'No need to go into details. Just take it easy, smile, and say "thank you". You'll be all right.'

Nevertheless, Lanie felt an embarrassed flush rising to her cheeks as she faced the huge audience. A thunder of applause rippled through the big room and she realised that a friendly-looking woman was pinning a mauve-coloured orchid to the shoulder of her white sun-frock. John Garfield's words reached her as from a distance. 'Much pleasure in awarding you the prize in our recent flour promotion contest ... one hundred shares——' he handed her a long white envelope and she smiled and said, 'Thank you.'

'And so that you can keep your hand in with the baking——' he handed her a second envelope. 'You can pick up the electric range at our warehouse right away if you wish.' More applause. Lanie found herself smiling back, saying 'thank you' all over again, then thankfully she escaped and made her way back towards her seat. As she threaded her way between the tables a sharp-faced woman of middle age rose to her feet. 'Do tell us, Miss Petersen, the secret of your winning bread recipe!'

Lanie's face felt stiff from forcing the smiles. 'I guess it's a bottle of beer!'

Amid more applause, John Garfield held up a hand and when the sound of clapping had died down, his voice could be heard. 'Not to worry, the recipe will appear on our packs of flour as from next month.' He appealed to the crowd of shareholders, all of whom were obviously enjoying the novelty of a light note amidst the mundane profit and loss accounts and long lists of figures, stock sheets and imports. 'Didn't she do well?'

'Well, thank goodness that's over!' Lanie dropped down into her seat and sipped the wine in its crystal goblet.

'That's fame for you.' Jim Sanderson was eyeing her with pride, almost as if she were his own Elaine.

She wrinkled her nose at him. 'Wasn't I lucky they didn't print my pictures on the flour packets as well as the recipe! But that huge electric range, do you think I should sell it?'

'I've got a better idea. How'd you like to take on a cooking job with me and my partner for three months? We could take you back with us to Rangimarie.'

The thoughts raced through Lanie's mind. She had taken a liking to this nice elderly farmer, and no doubt his partner would be just as agreeable. Two nice old guys who it would be easy to get on with. A faint hope stirred in her. Could she take this job? Dared she? After all, she could buy a cookery book, and she needed a job rather desperately right now.

She became aware that he was eyeing her attentively. 'It's only for a short time,' he urged, 'plain fare, no frills. You could handle it, no problem.'

She hesitated. 'It's awfully tempting to take you up on that offer but—you don't know what you're letting yourself in for.'

He waved her objection aside with a mahogany-tanned finger. 'We're used to that. Our Mrs. Hooper's a treasure, she's been with us for three years now and she's taking three months off to visit a sister in London. Before her time we had a succession of cooks, they came in all shapes and sizes and none of them lasted for long.'

A thought struck her. 'But how about your partner?'

'He won't worry. It will take a load off his mind, actually. That's one reason he came to town with me, to try and jack up a temporary cook. He's at the employment agency, worrying hell out of them, right now.'

'Supposing he's found someone already, some other woman with experience in the work? I'm not really a cook, you know.'

He grinned. 'Too bad, he'll just have to cancel the booking. Anyway, it would be some woman he'd never set eyes on before, an unknown quantity——'

Lanie dimpled. 'Like me?' As always in moments of indecision, she twisted a lock of shining hair round and round her finger. 'It does sound attractive, especially as I'm looking for country work and——'

'Your funds are running low?'

She looked up, surprised. 'Now how did you know that?'

He chuckled. 'The free meal today, remember?'

She laughed. 'But you don't seem to understand. I don't know a thing about real cooking. Just simple things I whipped up at the flat for Mary and me——'

He waved her misgivings aside. 'What the heck? You'll soon pick it up. Come on, give it a go!' There was an urgency about his tone that puzzled her. 'It's only for three months, after all.'

It was true, she thought. The job wasn't going to last for ever, and surely she could manage somehow. Two nice quiet elderlies. Probably they would be out working on the farm all day and there would be only one main meal to prepare in the evenings. A sheep farm ... they would be sure to live on mutton. All she need do would be to throw a roast in the oven each day or two.

'Ever done any riding, Lanie?' The masculine tones cut through her musing.

She raised a sparkling face. 'Have I ever? I love it. Of course I've only had weekends to ride. I don't even own a horse, but my friend Mary used to let me exercise her mare and ride at shows.'

'Swags of room to ride up in the hills at Rangimarie!'

Her face was alight with interest. 'I'd like that!' Her voice dropped to a puzzled note. 'Don't any experienced cooks want to work in the country?' she asked.

'We're a long way from civilisation, way back in the hills and fairly isolated. That means no social life to speak of, not much in the way of days off——'

'Oh, I wouldn't mind that!' Lanie's eyes shone with enthusiasm. 'It would all be new to me. If only——'

'You can practice on us. Sheep-farmers are a notoriously tough breed. We can take it.'

All at once she decided to take his advice and throw it over to fate. Her eyes were shining. 'I'll do it!'

'That's the spirit! Shake on it!' Jim Sanderson extended a sinewy arm and Lanie was about to grasp his extended hand when his arm fell limply and his head drooped. There was a grey tinge creeping around his mouth and she barely caught the words that fell from his lips. 'Pills . . . pocket.'

It all happened so swiftly that she acted compulsively. In a second she had leaped from her seat and was bending over him, feeling in the breast pocket of his jacket. With trembling fingers she found a small cardboard box, opened it and forced a pill between his lips. Thank heaven he retained consciousness sufficiently to swallow it, she thought, supporting him in her arms. After a moment or two a tinge of colour returned to his face and his eyelids fluttered open. His gaze focussed on her anxious face. 'Sorry,' he muttered, 'I must have flaked out for a moment.'

'You did! You gave me an awful fright, but luckily you told me you carried medication on you, and that was such a relief! Would you like me to call a doctor? There'll be a phone handy?'

'Lord no!' For a moment he looked distressed. 'Don't do that whatever you do!' He went on in a calmer tone, 'All I need is half an hour's rest and I'll be as good as new. I get these turns once in a while—a damned nuisance, but they don't last.'

'Let me take you back to your hotel, then?'

'No!' the word came explosively, 'that's the last thing I want! Not with Jard due back there at any moment!'

Lanie said, puzzled, 'But surely your partner will understand?'

'He won't get the chance.' His lips were set in a determined line. 'Not if I can help it!'

All at once she became aware of groups drifting towards the open doorway. 'Come along with me, then, and you can rest at the flat.' A taxi fare to the other end of town where she rented a modest bedsitter would make further inroads on her slender resources, but what matter?

Placing a guiding hand on Jim Sanderson's arm, she accompanied him to the lift and luckily, she thought, for her companion still looked rather groggy, she managed to flag down a taxi immediately. She helped him up the stairs and into her bedsitter, then flung open the windows with their view of the busy port of Auckland, while Jim Sanderson dropped thankfully down to a low couch. Lanie covered him with a light rug. 'How about a cuppa?' she suggested gently.

'Just what I need.' He spoke with closed eyes.

Moving into the tiny kitchen, she switched on the electric jug, but when she returned to the other room he was breathing deeply. Lanie let him sleep. Standing by the open window, she stared out to the sun-sparkled water where overseas liners lay alongside their berths. The suddenness of Jim Sanderson's heart attack, if that was what it had been, had driven everything else from her mind, but now she recalled his offer of a cooking job in the country. Would he mention it again when he awoke from sleep? she wondered.

As he had told her, half an hour's rest was all he needed to recover from the attack. He got to his feet, running a hand over tousled hair. 'Good of you to bother with me. Sorry to be such a nuisance.' All at once he was eyeing her with his penetrating gaze. 'Thought any more about that job offer of mine?' His voice took on an eager note. 'I'm hoping your answer is yes and we can take you back with us tomorrow. How does that strike you?'

Lanie's smile lighted up her small face. 'I think it's great! Always an enthusiast, she ran on happily. 'I've been looking for a job in the country and you need someone to help out in the kitchen department, so why not?'

He looked incredibly relieved at her words. 'That's the spirit, girl! Give it a go, I always say!'

The nice elderly partners must indeed be worried over their lack of staff in their home, she thought, for her companion to look so downright delighted at her acceptance of his offer of employment. If only they realised ... Honestly impelled her to say, 'I'm not a real cook, but if you don't mind my practising on you and your partner——'

'Not a bit. You'll pick it up in no time, you'll see.'

Seeing this was exactly the way she felt in the matter herself, Lanie nodded happily. Then a thought struck her. 'Your partner—he may have found someone suitable at the agency?'

'Not a hope! Unless they're working miracles in the employment line.'

'He won't mind—about me being young and all that?'

'Jard? Why should he? It'll be all the same to him. He'd planned to take someone back with him he didn't know from Adam, so what's the difference?' His lips twisted in a wry grin that she couldn't fathom. 'He doesn't know yet how lucky he is!'

'Lucky?'

He ignored the questioning note in her voice. 'You'll enjoy a spell on the station with us. It's big country, way back in the hills. We run sheep and cattle on the slopes and I grow maize down on the flats. Lately I've been having a go at growing sunflowers as well. Seems there's a good market for that sort of crop.'

'It all sounds fantastic!'

'Could be just what you're looking for. We pay good wages up at Rangimarie, well above award rates. You'd have decent quarters with a room to yourself, of course——' He broke off. 'I've just had a thought. Considering the state of your finances right now,' his hand went to the breast pocket of his jacket, 'how about something to go on with?'

'No—please——' Lanie stopped him with a determined shake of her head. 'I'd rather wait until everything is settled.' She smiled across at him. 'Not that I can see myself needing much money where I'm going. Are there any shops in the vicinity of Rangimarie?'

'Sorry, no stores, but not to worry.' Clearly he was apprehensive that she might change her mind about accepting the position. 'The boys are always taking a run into town for stores, stockfood, whatever. You won't be too cut off from civilisation.'

'Boys?' Alarm bells rang in her mind. 'Do they live with you?'

'Lord no. There are a couple of young shepherds on the place,' he explained. 'They've got single men's quarters and look after themselves.'

'Oh!' She breathed a sigh of relief. 'That's all right, then.'

'Right! Is one o'clock tomorrow afternoon okay for us to pick you up?'

'Oh yes, I'll be ready. I've only got my suitcase to pack——' She broke off, a hand to her mouth. 'My electric range, what'll I do about it?'

'Bring it along with you. There's swags of room in the truck. I'll get an electrician up from town to make the connection in the kitchen and you're away laughing! Give me the order on the warehouse and I'll see to it for you.'

Lanie fished in her handbag, then handed him the long envelope.

'Until tomorrow, then——' At the doorway he paused. 'Just one thing. About that little setback of mine today——' there was an odd evasive note in his voice, 'I'd be just as happy if you didn't let on to Jard about what happened today. I get these turns occasionally, but there's no need for him to know.'

'I understand just how you feel.' Lanie's eyes were sympathetic. 'I guess,' she hazarded, 'that he'd worry about you?'

A grin crossed the lined features. 'Something like that. So, not a word about my health, agreed?'

'Oh, you can trust me,' she assured him warmly. 'I won't say a thing!'

'Goodbye, then,' his tone deepened, 'and thanks for what you did today. You helped me a lot.'

' 'Bye, Mr. Sanderson——'

'Make it Sandy,' he grinned, and was gone.

Left alone, the thoughts tumbled wildly through Lanie's mind. Events had happened so swiftly. Was this the result of throwing it over to fate? Feeling all at once extraordinarily lighthearted, she set about cancelling her occupancy of the apartment. Then she phoned the few friends who would miss her when she'd gone. Her flatmate Mary was away on honeymoon, but the two other girls whom she contacted, although plainly astonished at Lanie's sudden decision to take on a cooking job in the country, wished her well. They would write to her, they promised, as soon as they were made aware of her new address.

Her new address! A thrill of excitement ran through her and she began jerking tops, dresses and slacks from hangers in the wardrobe and placing them in her suitcase. Lanie Petersen, she told herself, this is your chance at a whole new way of life! Enjoy!

CHAPTER TWO

CLEAR bright sunshine, streaming in at the open window, touched Lanie's face. For a few moments she lay dreaming, then her eyes flew open and as her gaze went to the empty wardrobe, the events of the previous day came rushing back to mind and she leaped from the bed.

She took a quick shower and decided that for the job she was about to take on, clothes were no problem. All she would need would be her well-worn blue denim jeans, thonged sandals and her supply of knitwear tops. She chose a white T-shirt with its printed motif running across the chest: THE TIME TO BE HAPPY IS NOW. Somehow the words seemed symbolic of the recent change in her fortunes. All at once her spirits were soaring. Could it be the golden morning, or was it the promise of an entirely new way of life, cooking meals for those two nice elderly farmers at their cosy property in the hills? Somehow she felt sure the farm would be of small acreage, just sufficient to keep both men pleasantly occupied. She imagined picture-book green paddocks surrounded by neat white paling fences enclosing a few grazing sheep and cattle, maybe a white goat to keep down the blackberries. The shabby little farm cottage would have tall hollyhocks leaning against the front fence and inside the dwelling there'd be comfortable worn chairs, old walnut chests, pipe racks along the mantel.

She decided that today she wouldn't use any make-up except for a touch of mascara to darken pale lashes. Her freckles would just have to show. Oh well, the nice elderlies were in need of a woman to cook their meals, heaven help them, not a beauty contest entrant.

She mixed a mug of instant coffee and slid bread into the toaster. Soon she had cleared away the light meal and went book shopping.

As she pushed the new cookery books she had bought an hour ago into her suitcase she reflected that she had everything she needed for her new position, except maybe a sun-hat. After all, it was still summer and she was bound for the country. Oh well, her denim cap would have to do. Planting it at a jaunty angle over her forehead, she pushed away tendrils of bright hair that had escaped from the knot on the top of her head. A glance in the mirror gave her a disquieting feeling that she didn't look one bit like a country cook. The term conjured up a plump and matronly-looking woman wearing a crisp white apron. No matter, she would just have to prove her worth, electric range and all! Think of it as a challenge, she encouraged herself. Sandy's got faith in me and that's a start. All I have to do now is to get on the right side of that partner of his.

At that moment, alerted by a sound on the street below, she glanced out of the window to see a sturdy utility pulling up outside. The vehicle could have nothing to do with her, she decided, for the driver was a young man, very attractive in a lean, sun-browned sort of way. She pulled aside the curtain for a second look— she couldn't help it, for he was the most attractive-looking male she had come across in a long time—that thatch of dark blond hair against the smooth tanned forehead, the strong features and deeply indented chin. But it wasn't just the way he looked, there was something about him, a vitality, an aliveness, that she could sense even at this distance.

It took her a moment or so to notice his companion, a thin figure seated beside the tall young man. Sandy! Apparently he was putting forward an argument, for he was flinging up work-lined hands, speaking quickly and defensively. Lanie couldn't hear what was being said, but it was evident that the two were involved in some dispute. But where, she wondered, was the nice elderly partner?

At that moment she glimpsed in the rear of the vehicle a gleam of white. So Sandy had already

collected the stove from the warehouse. Whatever the
subject of the disagreement it was clear that the
argument was becoming heated. Sandy's face had
turned to a deep brick-red beneath the tan and he was
thumping one fist angrily on to his palm. Crikey, Lanie
thought, in his state of health he'll do himself a mischief
if he goes on like that! Maybe I'd better go downstairs
and do something about it. At that moment, however,
the matter was resolved for her as the younger man—
goodness, he was tall, and so very erect—flung out of
the vehicle, his face stormy. 'Okay, okay,' he hadn't
raised his voice, yet the vibrant deep tones reached her
clearly, 'get this straight, it's not my idea!'

'Right, I'll take all responsibility!' Sandy had got out
of the utility. He was looking happier, almost smug, she
thought, having apparently gained a point in the
dispute with his passenger. Probably, she mused, the
younger man was a neighbour whom they were taking
back with them to the farming district where they all
lived. She wouldn't mind in the least being on the
journey with the wildly good-looking young man if only
he weren't in that black mood! Thank goodness it
wasn't herself who was the object of his anger! All at
once she caught the sound of footfalls on the stairs and
hurriedly she dropped the curtain back into place.
When Sandy tapped on the door a few minutes later she
welcomed him in with a smile, trying to look as though
she hadn't been a witness to the brief violent clash of
wills on the street below.

Sandy's lined brown face lighted up as he eyed her
suitcase. 'Good,' his tone was tinged with relief, 'you
haven't changed your mind about our little business
deal, then?'

She wrinkled her nose as she smiled up at him. 'Not if
you haven't had second thoughts about me.'

'Not a chance!'

'I'm all ready and waiting!' She took the mauve-
coloured orchid from its vase and bent to pick up her
suitcase. It wasn't heavy, but she knew Sandy wasn't a
fit man and there were the stairs to contend with.

'Give that to me!' A deep peremptory voice cut across her thoughts as a sun-tanned masculine hand took the case from her grasp. She glanced up in surprise to meet the chilliest grey eyes she had ever encountered. They were like cold steel, yet a fire seemed to burn in their depths, an icy dislike especially for her.

'Lanie Peterson,' Sandy was saying, 'my son Jardin.'

She was so taken aback that the words fell unbidden from her lips. 'But I got the idea that Mr Jardin——' what was she saying? she thought frantically—'was your partner?'

'That's right.' The stranger seemed to gloat over her discomfiture. 'I'll tell you something right now.' He towered above her, his muscular height intimidating enough without the taut angry set of his lips. 'My dad took it on himself to take you on without a word to me about it. I'm warning you that' as from now I'll do the hiring,' his off-putting expression lent significance to the words, 'and the firing!'

All at once it came to Lanie that it was she who had been the cause of that bitter argument down there in the utility, and a flame of anger shot through her at the thought. Who did he think he was, for heaven's sake, this arrogant young farmer from the backblocks? She didn't *have* to do as he said. She stood very straight and lifted her small rounded chin. 'Your father offered me the job of cook on your farm. If you don't want me to have the position I don't need to come. I'm not sure that I want the job anyway!'

She saw his angry glance challenge the older man in a silent battle of wills.

'It was only a suggestion,' she said with spirit. 'I happened to be on the look-out for some work in the country——'

'Like a typing job in the outback?' His lip curled contemptuously. 'Don't give me that!'

The low muttered words were scarcely audible. What was the matter with him? Why did he mistrust her so? A dark cloud of anger mushroomed up inside her, but she forced her voice to calmness, only the heightened colour

that had risen to her cheekbones betraying her feelings.
'Your dad let me in on the job offering at your property
at Rangimarie——' Luckily she had memorised the soft
Maori syllables.

'That's right,' Sandy agreed. 'I told Lanie the job was
hers if she wanted it.'

Once again she intercepted a brief clash of glances
between eyes of a lively brown and a flint-like grey.
Then Jard said tightly, 'If it's a promise, then that's it!'

At that moment the shrill ring of the telephone rang
through the room and Lanie bent to pick up the
receiver.

'Lanie!' Trevor's deep tones, ragged with emotion,
came over the wire. 'Just thought I'd give you a ring to
see if you'd changed your mind about me, about us?'

'No, I haven't.' She was acutely aware of the
watchful silence around her. She had a suspicion that
the masculine tones were all too audible to the two men
in the small room with her. 'Everything's just the same,'
she said quickly. 'Trevor, I've got to go! I'm just
leaving. I'm taking some work out of town——'

'But you can't go, just like that! Where can I get in
touch with you? What——'

'Goodbye!' She slammed down the receiver and
turned a flushed face to meet Jard's impassive stare. He
said coolly, 'If it's not convenient for you——'

'Oh, it is! It is!' It was the way he was looking at her,
she thought hotly, that was making her feel flustered,
causing her to run on quickly, nervously. 'It was no one
important. Just a man I used to be engaged to.'

His thick dark eyebrows rose and his expression was
colder than ever, if that were possible. 'I get it.' Lanie
wondered wildly how it was that the commonplace
words could convey a whole world of distrust. 'Let's go,
shall we?'

Lanie held her ground, her green eyes shooting
sparks in his direction. Somehow she managed to school
her tone to a light, uncaring note. 'If you're quite sure
you want me to come with you?'

'*Want you?*' The words he flung at her were aimed to

hurt. His obvious reluctance to have her along today had the effect of making her all the more determined to oppose him. He had no right to order everyone around as obviously he was in the habit of doing. It was high time that this arrogant, autocratic male was taught a lesson, and after all, what had she to lose? She had half a mind to call the whole thing off, but she wanted this job and if it entailed enduring the unfounded dislike of Sandy's overbearing son—well, she could cope! She was tempted to poke out her tongue at the sardonic, mocking face. Instead she pushed her cap further down over one eye and said challengingly, 'Suits me.'

If only he wasn't so wildly attractive! The crazy thought shot through her mind as she preceded the two men down the stairs.

Seated in the utility with its long front seat, Lanie found herself squeezed between Jard and his father. Now that the decision had been made she found a curious satisfaction in the thought that, like it or not, Jard was lumbered with her seated close beside him on the long journey ahead. She flung him a quick sideways glance, and as she took in the angry line of his lips she couldn't resist saying, 'Sorry I'm not fair, fat and forty!' Her wide happy smile that invariably made immediate impact on masculine companions had no effect on him whatever. She tried once again. 'Is that what you put an order in for at the employment agency?'

'It's not a matter of looks,' he grated, 'and it's nothing to do with me!'

He shot her a glance and her soft lips firmed. She wasn't done with him yet, she vowed silently. He deserved something in the way of retaliation, the way he was treating her.

'Thanks for picking up the range for me,' she murmured sweetly.

His lips twitched at the corners, but not with humour. 'All part of the service, not my idea. There's nothing wrong with the electric stove at home that I can see. Of all the crazy ideas! First time I ever came across a cook who carted her stove around the country with her!'

'Maybe you haven't met many of the species,' she murmured. 'Anyway, what else could I do with it?'

'Sell the damned thing. Give it away!'

At least, she thought, she had provoked him into speech. She affected a hurt note in her voice. 'Oh, I couldn't do that! It's the only prize I've ever won in my life!'

'Dad put me in the picture about it.' His voice was deadpan. 'According to him, you're Miss Supercook— quite a reputation to have. Let's hope,' he drawled, 'you'll be able to live up to it!'

The beast, she fumed inwardly, the hateful sarcastic beast! She would need to disillusion him on that score or she would really find herself in difficulties. She took a deep breath. 'Actually, I'm not really——'

'Three hundred miles to go! I take it you've never been down to our part of the country, Lanie?' Sandy's voice, louder than she had previously heard it, cut across her soft tones.

'Never.'

'It will be all new territory to you, then. A change of scenery as well as work?'

'I guess so,' she agreed. 'A kind of holiday,' and out of a corner of her eye caught Jard's satirical glance. What was the matter with the man? A gorgeous-looking male like that must have been utterly spoiled by women, she mused. In view of the cooking situation on the farm, he was unmarried. Small wonder! No girl of today would put up with his autocratic ways. This particular girl loathed him, and that was just what he was in need of by the look of things, a level-headed girl like herself who happened to be immune to his forceful domination.

The odd thing was that, hating him as she did, she had this *awareness* of his nearness, and she had to admit that his attraction was breathtaking. So lithe and muscular, with eyes that said more than his lips (unfortunately for her). And whoever started that mistaken idea that only dark men were attractive? She stole a sideways glance towards him as he swung the vehicle into a long line of city traffic. The clinging fabric of his cream body-shirt revealed the rippling muscles of broad shoulders and his strong profile was worth looking at (that was, of course, if you didn't happen to know the man!) Oh yes, he was good-looking enough to be any girl's dream, but not this girl! She admitted he had something, a male charisma that was shattering. Even she could feel it, but fortunately she was forewarned against that particular snare.

Swept by conflicting emotions, she had been all but oblivious of her surroundings. Now, however, she realised they were taking a motorway leading out of the city and bright with its centre strip of flowering shrubs, scarlet bottle-brush and delicately tinted blossoms of oleanders. Presently the suburban homes of pastel shadings clustered on either side of the *toi-toi*-bordered road gave way to sundried paddocks with grazing sheep and cattle, and soon they had left the motorway to take the main road south.

Lanie made no effort to break the silence that had fallen as they left the city boundaries behind. Why should she bother to talk to a man who was so definitely antagonistic towards her? After a while she became aware of Sandy's enthusiastic tones.

'You'll enjoy the climate down our way, Lanie. No clouds in the sky, just the clear sunshine day after day. Once you've tried our air up in the hills you'll never want to come back to town!'

Flicking a swift glance towards Jard's uncommunicative face, however, she wasn't so sure on that point. Aloud she said smilingly, 'I'll take your word for it!'

Sandy went on to describe life in the country region for which they were bound, but Lanie was scarcely aware of what he was saying. There was something about Jard that was definitely disturbing, especially when she found herself pressed close to his lean muscular body, conscious in spite of herself of a masculine magnetism that operated regardless of her positive loathing for the man! With an effort she wrenched her random thoughts aside and tried to concentrate on Sandy's voice. What was he saying? Something about her new job?

'You'll get along fine and if you have any problems, Clara will soon sort them out for you.'

'Clara?' she queried.

'She's our housekeeper, and a jolly good sort too. She's been with us for donkey's years.'

'Oh!' Her thoughts were busy. A housekeeper *and* a cook! Somehow it didn't line up with the cottage on the farm.

'She's one of the family, just about,' Sandy was saying, and Lanie gave a sigh of relief. Clara was no doubt a family friend who had made her home with them and to whom they had given the nominal title of housekeeper. For a moment there she had known a prickle of apprehension.

All at once it occurred to her that she didn't know anything, not anything, of what she was letting herself in for at the end of this journey, not for sure that is. A glance towards Jard's clean-cut profile did nothing to ease her misgivings. Plainly he was furious about her being taken on to work for him and his father and wasn't troubling to hide his displeasure. Lanie wasn't all that keen on the idea of the new job herself, not since she had learned of the antipathy of Sandy's 'partner'. What had he expected? A portly motherly type of woman with her hair in a bun and no make-up? She giggled to herself. At least the last two attributes applied to her! Her mercurial spirits rose. And then there was Sandy, she had a champion in him. Something told her that for some reason she didn't understand, Jard's opposition in the matter of her employment had no effect whatever on his father. On the contrary.

They sped on, passing at intervals small townships with their scattering of houses on either side of the main road. The hot sun was making spangles on the windscreen and everywhere was the dry scent of wildflowers and summer. Soon they were in sight of the little town of Te Kauwhata with its roadside stalls of luscious fruit, purple grapes, big yellow peaches, apples and pears. 'No need to stop here,' Sandy told her, 'there's swags of fruit in the orchard at home—kiwi fruit, avocado pears, the lot!'

'Sounds fantastic!' Privately the thought went through her mind that she would need a lot more than a supply of fresh fruit to compensate for working for the man with his hands on the driving wheel.

Presently they dropped down a slope to follow the course of the Waikato river, wide and clear with its moored sand barges and willow-shaded banks.

All at once they were in sight of bush-covered hills piercing the limpid blue of the sky and she knew they were approaching the town of Ngaruawahia with its swiftly-flowing river and high hills. On the highest peak of all was the burial place of Maori kings. It was as they approached the long graceful bridge spanning the swiftly-flowing green depths below that Lanie caught an unusual sound in the car motor. An enquiring glance in Sandy's direction brought the response that he too had noticed it.

'It's been missing on and off for a while,' Jard told her. 'Could be the coil's not doing its job, but it's more likely to be the ignition.' He was pulling in to the side of the road as he spoke and cars and trucks sped past them.

Lanie watched as the two men got out of the vehicle and Jard flung open the bonnet to peer inside. 'Doesn't look to be anything particularly wrong.'

'Just what I was thinking.'

At least they appeared to be on good terms again, she reflected. It seemed it was the sight of her that had caused Jard to lash out at everyone in sight. Well, so long as she was warned he would find it no easy matter to push her around. For some reason she couldn't understand, he seemed to have a preconceived opinion of her. If only she knew what had put him in that frame of mind, she would know better how to deal with him—

her soft lips tightened, for deal with him she would. It wasn't for nothing she had been born with flame-coloured hair.

At last Jard slammed down the bonnet of the vehicle. 'I'll take it in to the next garage and let them have a look.' When they drew in to the garage, however, a mechanic told him that it would be a matter of testing the coil. Everyone in the place was flat-stick today. As he spoke vehicles were crowding in to the small space. It was the busiest day of the year for the garage with the Regatta Day crowds and vehicles needing attention, but he'd do his best. If they could call back in an hour or so?

Of course, Lanie mused, the Regatta at Ngaruawahia, the day when the seafaring tradition of famous Polynesian sea voyages came to life again at the annual Maori Aquatic Carnival held on the grassy banks of the Waikato River. It was an event she had never attended, and she had a sneaky wish that the truck repairs would hold them up sufficiently for her to take in the river races and Maori culture competitions. Even from this distance she caught a glimpse of long canoes paddled by enthusiastic young Maori men. The blare of loudspeakers mingled with the shouts and cheering of the watching crowd gathered on the river banks and brightly-coloured sun-umbrellas blossomed like flowers among tents and side-shows. She would like to view the events—and what a welcome respite the visit would be from Jard's disturbing presence!

The stern set of his jaw told her he had no wish for the journey to be prolonged. She bet, though, that he would have felt differently in the matter had he not been forced to have her along as his passenger on the trip. Sandy's pleasant tones seemed to tune in on her thoughts. 'You can drop Lanie and me down at the river. We may as well have a look at the Regatta, seeing we have to fill in time.'

'Right!' He spoke with alacrity and Lanie thought, 'He can't wait to get rid of me, even temporarily. Well, that goes for me too!'

They merged into the long line of traffic moving towards the small town with its backdrop of bushclad hills, violet-hazed on slopes away from the sun. Presently Jard drew up on the grassy reserve and Lanie and Sandy got out of the vehicle to join the holiday crowds that lined the banks of the swiftly-flowing river.

'Aren't we lucky,' she smiled up at Sandy, 'to be just in time for the highlight of the day!' For over a loudspeaker came the announcement of the grand parade of the war canoes, the *waka taua*.

He nodded. 'Now you can see the clock turn back for a hundred years——' At that moment his words were drowned by a wild cheering as the three great canoes swept downriver, the young Maori paddlers working in time to the rhythmic commands of their captain, the *kai-tuki*, standing amidships.

The giant canoes with their intricately carved figureheads at stern and prow jostled for a lead, then, to the enthusiastic encouragement of the onlookers, the leading canoe swept on to victory. A race of smaller canoes followed, and Lanie laughed with the crowd around them as canoes raced over hurdles and occupants were spilled into the water.

Afterwards they made their way among the picnic groups and from a small Maori boy Sandy bought luscious slices of pinky-silver watermelon nestling in a woven flax basket.

Still biting into the crisp cool slice of melon, she strolled on with Sandy and they paused to watch the wood-chopping competition. Afterwards Lanie's attention was drawn to a barge moored in the clear green river where dark-haired Maori maidens wearing the traditional flax skirts and *taniko* patterned headband sang and danced in rhythmic movements, their quivering hands simulating the shimmering of the summer's heat haze.

It was really entertaining, she thought, the aquatic events and side-shows, all in this happy holiday atmosphere. She should be enjoying it so much, and she was in a way, yet somehow she saw the events taking place around her with only half her attention. And why? Because Jard's sardonic face intruded on her thoughts and refused to be dispelled. She couldn't seem to get him out of her mind.

At that moment, as if conjured up out of her thoughts, she realised he was making his way purposefully through scattered groups to come to stand beside them.

'Well,' Sandy enquired, 'what's the verdict?'

His son looked, she thought, more angry than ever, if that were possible. 'No good ... seems it's a faulty coil right enough. They haven't got one to fit in stock, the big day here has seen to that, and they tell me the best they can do is to send to Hamilton and get one out in the morning.'

For a moment Sandy looked worried, then he shrugged his shoulders philosophically. 'Can't be helped. The only problem is,' his eyes swept the crowded scene surging around them, 'there won't be a motel unit vacant anywhere for miles, not tonight.'

'It's okay, I managed to get a cancellation. I've left the bags there. I'll take you over there right now if you like, it's just over the other side of the river.'

His tone was tinged with a hidden implication Lanie couldn't fathom. Unless—— Surely he couldn't have the crazy idea that his father had a personal interest in her, from which he had to be rescued? She brushed the thought away as too absurd to entertain. She became aware that Sandy was saying with a grin, 'How do you feel about it, Lanie? Have you seen enough of the show for today?'

She nodded in agreement, but underneath her thoughts were churning wildly. It seemed that only one of her male escorts showed some common consideration in asking her if she wanted to leave the colourful scene. As they made their way through the crowd in the direction of the parking area, Jard made no attempt to query her enjoyment of the display of Maori singing and dancing or even the race of the war canoes. He didn't ask her a thing, but confined his remarks to

Sandy. To Jard, she thought heatedly, apparently I don't exist! No doubt he wishes I didn't! If she found herself forced to spend the remainder of the day in his reluctant company she didn't know how she was going to endure it.

It transpired, however, that the ordeal was to be spared her. For after showing her to her room in the attractively arranged motel unit, he left her with the suggestion that they all meet by arrangement that evening in the dining room.

Later in the day, Lanie changed out of her denim jeans and cotton top. She was having distinct reservations concerning that 'time to be happy is now' motif printed on her T-shirt. Whoever thought that one up, she mused crossly, had never met a man like Jard Sanderson, that was for sure! Taking from her suitcase a soft clinging silk dress in the one delicate shade of pink a redhead can wear successfully, she slipped her feet into white high-heeled sandals and surveyed with some satisfaction the effect of her soft green eye-shadow. At the dinner table in the crowded restaurant room, however, she told herself that she didn't know why she had bothered with her appearance. So far as Jard was concerned, he did his best to ignore her, and she sensed that Sandy, loyally endeavouring to make up for his son's ill humour, was finding the effort heavy going. To Lanie it was a relief when coffee was brought to the table and the meal came to an end. Shortly afterwards, on the excuse of giving herself an early night, she escaped to her room.

Her cheeks still burned from the touch of the sun beating down on the crowds at the river bank that afternoon and making her now feel drowsy. Tonight she felt that in spite of the upsets of the day she would fall asleep easily. That was, of course, if she didn't allow herself to dwell on thoughts of Jard. He made her so *mad*!

She took a shower, then slipped into cool cotton pyjamas of a pink-and-white striped pattern. Then settling herself back on the pillow she flung her long

plait of hair back over her shoulder and picked up the
paperback novel she had brought with her. Somehow,
thought, the words danced before her eyes and the
story-line failed to hold her interest. Instead she found
herself pondering on the fact that invariably in
romantic novels when the hero for one reason or
another came bursting unexpectedly into the girl's
room, she was always attired in see-through garments
of provocative appeal, like a float-away negligee. On
neither count would that ever happen to her, she
mused, then stiffened as a peremptory rat-a-tat sounded
on the door.

'Who is it?' she called guardedly.

'It's me, Jard!' she caught the note of suppressed
anger in the low vibrant tones, 'and you'd better let me
in! I've got things to say to you, *and* without the old
man putting in his say!'

For a moment she hesitated, then 'Oh, all right,
then.' Moving to the door, she flung it open and he
towered above her, dominant, erect and menacing. It
was clear that he meant business. 'You'd better take a
seat,' she gestured towards the bed.

He shook his head impatiently. 'I can say what I
want to right here!' At the hostility in his tone Lanie
braced herself for the coming attack. This was war!

'Now look here,' she said defiantly, 'if you're on
again about my taking on the job with you and your
dad——'

His thick dark eyebrows rose satirically. 'How did
you guess?'

She ignored the sarcasm in his tone. 'It wasn't my
idea!'

He pinned her with his hard accusing gaze. 'Are you
telling me I can't believe the evidence of my eyes?'

'I don't care what you believe!' Anger was welling up
inside her. 'It was Sandy who offered me the job!'

'So it's Sandy, is it? Quick work, wasn't it, Miss
Petersen?'

With an effort she crushed down the black tide of
fury that threatened to overspill. 'We got on fine

together right from the start, and he asked me to call him that.'

His lips curled. 'I'll bet he did! I suppose you'll tell me next that this,' he swung around to pluck the orchid from its vase on the mantel, 'isn't another of his happy thoughts?'

'Put that down!' She snatched the frail blossom from his grasp. 'Of all the——' She broke off, lost for words. 'For your information,' with an effort she forced her voice to a cool and collected note, 'it was given to me at the shareholders' meeting of the flour company when they presented me with the competition prize.'

'So *you* say!' He eyed her disbelievingly, but the next moment the indignation blazing her in green eyes must have got through to him, for he muttered a low, 'Sorry, I got the wrong idea——'

'Yes, you have!' Swiftly she grasped the opportunity he had handed to her. 'Just like you've got the wrong idea about everything else . . . about me.'

'Really?' he drawled. 'You'd better put me in the picture, then. The old man isn't usually interested in females, young or old. I'd be interested to know just how you got around him so quickly——' His narrowed gaze swept over her flushed young face, then moved down to the smooth tanned skin at the base of her throat exposed by the deep V of her pyjama jacket. 'Apart from the way you look, of course, that could account for a lot!'

Taken by surprise, she knew only one emotion, a hot and blinding anger. How dared he, how dare he treat her this way, taking it for granted that coming to work on his property was entirely her idea, as if she had engineered the whole affair? 'Look,' she cried defensively, 'you're all wrong about me! You're way out and you may as well know it right now! Sandy——'

'Oh yes, Sandy——'

At the derisive curl of his lips she had to hold her breath while she got control of her runaway emotions. At last she said stiffly, 'We got to talking at the meeting and when I told him I was on the look-out for a country job he mentioned that there was work offering at his place. It seemed a good idea, and when he was with me at the flat——' She broke off abruptly, aghast at Jard's expression. The way he was looking at her, the cynical light in his eyes! He couldn't be thinking that for purposes of her own she had deliberately set out to trap an elderly man into friendship, or even a more intimate association? But of course she could explain the visit to her bedsitter quite simply—or could she? Across her mind flashed a picture of Sandy's pale, oddly intent face. 'You won't let on to Jard about what happened to me today?'

The cold accusing tones fell across her musing. 'And don't try to tell me the old boy had a heart attack or something of the sort, because it won't wash! He's as strong as can be and as wiry as hell! You'll have to think up something better than that to convince me!'

As she hesitated, Lanie became aware of the relentless tones. 'He's a nice old boy, my dad, trusting old guy. It must have been the easiest thing in the world for you to get away with it.' His tone hardened. 'But you won't find it so easy to pull the wool over my eyes. And contrary to what you might be thinking, what I say goes! Just,' he bent on her his deep formidable gaze, 'don't go messing about with the old boy's feelings. Right now he's so bemused with his new little friend he'd make himself believe anything. Oh, you might have made a fool of my dad, but that baby face and sweet husky voice doesn't fool me one little bit!'

She was all but choking with fury. She said very low, *'Get out of my room!'*

He made no move to go. 'Don't worry, I will, once I've put the record straight. The old man's so besotted with you he's even got you mixed up in his mind with my sister. Actually his Elaine is quite a different type of girl, thank the Lord. You can trust *her!*'

Lanie was very pale. 'But not me? Is that what you're trying to say?'

His eyes were cold fire. 'You know the answer to that one.'

Suddenly the wild anger that had been boiling up inside her spilled over and, scarcely aware of her action, her hand flew out as she stretched upwards and with all the power she could summon, delivered a stinging blow to his cheek. It was satisfying, she thought hotly, to see the red marks of her fingers imprinted on his darkly tanned face. Breathing hard, she eyed him defiantly, but beyond an involuntary flinch at her blow, he betrayed no particular reaction.

'It wasn't like you think!' she cried once again. Heavens, what was he thinking? That she had manoeuvred an elderly man into offering her the farm job? She looked up at him, taking in the hard unyielding lines of his tanned face. 'You don't know anything about me! It's all lies——'

His bark of laughter held no amusement. 'Did I accuse you of anything?'

'Not in so many words, but——'

'Why not let me in on it, then?' His voice was rapier-sharp. 'Go ahead, I'm listening.'

'Ask your father yourself, if you're so damned suspicious about me,' she countered.

The twist to his lips held no amusement. 'I did, and he's mighty evasive about the whole thing. He's a softie in some respects, anyone can take him in by playing on his sympathies——'

'Well, I didn't!' she flashed. Taking a deep breath, she caught her lower lip in her teeth to stop the trembling. 'All right, then, if that's the way you feel about me, you don't have to employ me——'

'Don't tempt me!' His savage tones cut across her soft husky accents. After a second's pause the harsh tones went on. 'Unfortunately, though I manage the station, and my dad's made Rangimarie over to me, he still has some say in the running of the show. For reasons of his own he's given you the job and that's it, but,' his voice dropped to a low formidable note, 'get this. You'd better pull your weight around the place or you'll find yourself out on your ear so soon you'll wonder what's hit you! Another thing,' he held her with his implacable gaze. 'The way the old man's talking, you're Miss Supercook, Cordon Bleu, the lot!' The cold tones lashed out at her. 'You scarcely look the part!' His cool gaze raked her small slender figure.

'What?' Lanie eyed him incredulously. She had taken in only the first part of what he had told her. 'But I didn't tell him anything of the sort!' she protested hotly. 'I made it plain to him that I wasn't——'

'Well then,' came the hatefully mocking tones, 'it's up to you, isn't it?'

'And you're hoping like mad,' she flashed, 'that I'll make an unholy mess of things!'

'Did I say so?'

'You didn't need to spell it out.' She faced him with all the dignity she could muster—difficult when she barely came to his shoulder and he was so big. He was also the most maddening man she had ever come across in her life! 'I mightn't be the world's top cook,' she flung at him, 'but it's all lies, the things you're hinting at about me and Sandy!'

His eyes narrowed thoughtfully. 'Is it now? I wonder?' All at once he had caught her bare arm in a hurtful grip. 'You tell me you're a cook, pure and simple and I say you're nothing but a little opportunist, that you were on the make and when you saw a chance you took it——'

'Let me go!'

He took not the slightest notice of her struggles to free her arm from his painful grip. 'Get this straight!' He towered above her, setting her trembling. 'If you're going to work for me, *you'd better be good*!' At last he released her.

Lanie rubbed her arm where his savage clasp had pressed into her soft flesh. 'You don't have to worry yourself about me,' she cried breathlessly, 'I'll get a bus back to town in the morning!'

Jard held her defiant green gaze with his formidable glance.

'No, you won't! I'm not having the old man upset at this stage of the game!'

'Too bad.' She scarcely knew what she was saying, with the anger boiling up inside her and exploding in a black cloud. She never knew she could hate anyone so much! 'Let me tell you something!' she flung at him. 'On second thoughts I've changed my mind about going back to town. I can't wait to show you just how mistaken you can be about people—about me!'

He sent her his hateful twisted smile. 'Great!' She knew by the sarcasm he put into the word that he simply didn't believe her capable of proving herself to him, and the thought sparked her to throw him a challenging glance. 'You might be surprised!'

His glance was definitely off-putting, but he merely remarked coolly, 'I might at that.' Then turning swiftly on his heel, he moved with his easy stride towards the door, and closed it behind him.

Through a mist of unshed tears Lanie gazed down at the red marks on her arm where his strong fingers had pressed into the flesh. She was still trembling. Nothing, she vowed, but nothing would stop her now from going on with this mad venture. She would prove Jard mistaken in his horrible misguided opinion of her, even if it took her the whole three months of her stay at Rangimarie to accomplish it. She didn't know how she was going to convince him, she only knew she would. It would be worth working as a cook on his farm, worth anything, she told herself, if at the end of it all she could force that arrogant man to admit how wrong, wrong, wrong he had been in his snap judgment of her.

That night it was a long time before she could get to sleep as over and over again the angry thoughts tumbled through her mind. Jard was so convinced in his mind that she was a conniving adventurer, out for all she could get. Oh, she could kill that man! Viciously she flung her pillow over and punched it.

She had dreaded the meeting with Jard in the restaurant, but when in the morning she went down to breakfast it was Sandy who awaited her at the door. 'I thought you'd be along any moment now.' Freshly shaved and alert, he looked as pleased to see her, the thought flashed through her mind, as if she were his own Elaine. It was very odd. She brought her mind back to the masculine tones. 'Jard breakfasted ages ago, then took off for the garage.' The shrewd gaze took in the dark smudges around Lanie's eyes. 'Sleep all right last night, lass?'

'Yes, fine, thank you.'

'That's good.' He gave the waitress an order for cornflakes, toast and coffee, then turned on her his penetrating gaze. 'Not having second thoughts about that cooking job with us, are you?'

She hesitated. 'Actually . . .' Her voice trailed away. In view of last night's stormy encounter with his son it was difficult to make her smile bright and convincing.

'Because if you happen to have any notions in that direction I'm warning you right now that I'm going to do my damnedest to talk you out of them.' He met her troubled glance. 'Something bothering you, is there?'

She decided to come right out with it. Choosing her words carefully, she said slowly, 'It's just your son. He's definitely against the whole idea of my taking on the job with you.'

'Did he tell you that?' He shot the question at her, but she parried it neatly. 'He had no need to spell it out. He wishes me anywhere else in the world but on the way to Rangimarie. Anyone can see that. It's the way he looks at me, and all the things he *doesn't* say! I know he thinks I'm too young and inexperienced, and I guess,' she smiled across the table, 'when you come right down to it, he could be right!'

'Rubbish, lass!' You'll make out fine, you'll see! Just give it a go! Don't worry about Jard,' he grinned, 'it'll do him a power of good not to get his way all of the time. He'll come around after a while, you can take my word for it.'

She flicked him a disbelieving glance from under her lashes. 'With my cooking and the way he feels about me?'

'Oh, come on, lass,' his tone was encouraging, 'you mustn't let him bother you. Just give him time.'

'But he's so angry!' She bit her lip thoughtfully. 'I wouldn't like to be the cause of any trouble between you——'

'You can put that idea right out of your mind, lass.' His hearty laugh dispelled her misgivings. 'Just because nowadays he happens to manage the show, it doesn't mean we don't have our little management difficulties and differences! Come on now,' the twinkling brown eyes were entreating, 'you're not the girl I took you for if you're going to let my son scare you away from Rangimarie before you've had a stab at the job.' All at once his voice took on a serious note. 'You're not thinking of giving it away and going back to town today, are you? Not already? Just because of Jard?'

Jard. The name had the power to stir her to a wild anger and fierce determination. What had she been thinking of? Running away, giving in to his dominating ways? Meekly acceding to his demands? Demands based on his own entirely mistaken interpretation of the relationship that existed between his father and herself. She'd take that job, and what was more, she vowed silently, she'd be so darned good at it that Jard would be forced to admit how mistaken he had been in his snap judgment of her. She couldn't *wait* for the moment of truth when she would accept his apology for the hurtful, high-handed treatment he had handed out to her. Lost in her exciting dream of the future, she took a moment or so for Sandy's anxious tones to register in her mind.

'You're not thinking of turning it in, lass?'

Lanie sent him a smile that was quite dazzling, a smile full of confidence and hope. 'Not on your life!'

CHAPTER THREE

It should have been an enjoyable journey, Lanie mused as they sped south down the winding highway with its long stretches of farmlands and the occasional small settlement comprising a cluster of timber houses, a garage, a general store and old hotel, built alongside the road. It would have been pleasant travelling too, she thought resentfully, had it not been for the closed masculine profile she could glimpse from a corner of her eye. If only she didn't have this odd *awareness* of him. Why couldn't she be like Sandy, who, apparently unmindful of his son's off-putting silence, was cheerfully pointing out to her the features of the various areas through which they were passing.

Was Jard always so grim and uncommunicative, she wondered, or could it be she who had upset him? She could almost feel his disapproval and antagonism. *You know the answer to that one!* The errant thought shot through her mind that she could put up with his silent displeasure, but it was very hard to fight against this crazy awareness of his physical nearness. Thank heavens he had no way of knowing her feelings in that direction.

Lost in her thoughts, she scarcely took in the road cut through vast pine plantations on which they were travelling, or the notices on the trees, 'Young pines growing. Take care.'

They had journeyed a long way towards their destination when Lanie, gazing idly out of the window, suddenly caught her breath, forgetting everything else, even for a moment the man close at her side, in her first glimpse of Mount Egmont. Cloud-shadowed, the symmetrical cone reached into the translucent sky, snow-capped even in the heat of summer. The misty shape of the mountain seemed to travel with them as they followed the coastline and the miles fell away.

Small towns flashed by the windows of the vehicle. Patea with its blue-roofed farmhouses and macrocarpa-lined road, its sculptured model of a carved Maori canoe set high above the municipal hall.

'Finest dairy land in the island coming up,' Sandy told her as they looked out on lush green paddocks studded with grazing cattle. Lanie roused herself to say laughingly, 'I never thought the T.V. commercials for cheese factories down this way were real, the sky so blue, grass so green—not until now.'

Presently they were passing high sandhills, the dark sand glittering in the sunshine. Lanie caught brief glimpses of sun-sparkle on water, distant views of rocky headlands and the white surf rolling in from the Tasman.

Dusk was falling when at last Jard swung the vehicle off the main highway and into a metalled side road. They sped down into a punga-filled gully then climbed a road winding over vast, sheep-threaded hills. Long shadows of overhanging bush lay across the road as they moved deeper into the hills and a purple haze filled the gullies. Lanie caught swift impressions of roadside notices, Wandering Stock, Beware Falling Debris. Then Jard was swinging the truck around a sharp bend, slowing speed to guide the vehicle past a drover on horseback, with his dogs. As they followed the lonely highway she caught an occasional glimpse of the sea, a darkening blue triangle between the hills. Through the gathering gloom she made out the outlines of sheep-drafting pens at the gates of long, poplar-lined drives leading up to lighted farmhouses high on dark slopes.

As they swept on the headlamps of the truck illuminated a fragment of the winding road ahead, pinpointing the body of a possum trapped by the deadly attraction of lights in the darkness. Had it not been for Jard's disturbing presence Lane would have been lulled into a half doze, but his close proximity kept her all too conscious of him, every single minute.

It was a long time since they had passed any lighted

farmhouses and she could discern no sign of civilisation, only the dark outlines of bush-clad hills closing in around them. At that moment a battered signpost loomed up out of the gloom and in the glare of the headlamps she made out the faded lettering, Rangimarie. They swung into a rough track and Lane peered into the darkness, but still she could see no sign of lights.

'Nice-sounding Maori name,' she said brightly, and turned towards Jard. She would *make* him say something to her, she vowed. 'What does it mean?'

'*Rangi*, the sky-father,' ice dripped in his tone, '*marie*, peace.'

'Peace!' she echoed incredulously, and tried to subdue the bubble of laughter that rose to her lips. 'Oh *no*! It's hardly appropriate right now, do you think?' She couldn't resist the jibe, and after all, Jard could scarcely send her back to town, not at this point of the journey. 'Is that really the translation?'

He refused to be drawn. A flat, 'So the local Maoris tell me,' tossed in her direction and that was all. He didn't even spare her a sideways glance. Oh, she might have known! Better to ignore the man and concentrate on Sandy, who clearly was only too eager to welcome her to his home. She smiled up at him. 'Rangimarie. Is that the name of your district?'

Sandy's chuckle exploded in the darkness. 'You could put it that way, eh, Jard? Name of our place, actually.'

'Oh!' Still under the spell of the novelty of her surroundings, she said in her warm husky voice, 'We'll soon be reaching your cottage, then?' A belated sense of politeness impelled her to add, 'Yours and Jard's, I mean.'

Unthinkingly her gaze moved to Jard and to her surprise she saw that he was looking amused. Only it wasn't a real grin that touched his mouth, it was more in the nature of a sardonic lift of the lips at some thought of his own. What had she said wrong, for heaven's sake? All at once she wasn't sure of her ground. Panic touched her with a chill finger. This dark

lonely road at the edge of nowhere with no sign of
civilisation in sight. And she was here with two
strangers. Just what, she wondered, had she let herself
in for? She said uncertainly, 'You do both live just
around here somewhere?'

'Sure, sure we do.' Sandy's chuckle was reassuring to
her taut nerves. 'The old place will be coming up pretty
soon now, right at the end of the drive.'

They rumbled over a cattlestop and she strained her
eyes into the darkness, dimly making out the road
ahead. At that moment she caught in her nostrils the
salt tang of the sea. So the cottage was situated
somewhere near the coast. Goody, goody, things were
looking up!

What a long distance the dwelling must be from the
main road, she mused, for as yet she could discern no
sign of any dwellings. Stones thudded against the
undercarriage of the truck as they moved on, and the
next minute she realised they were passing the dim
outlines of outbuildings, stockyards and stables. And
surely those faint lights were shining from the
windows of two cottages? The next moment they
swung around a curve in the track and the headlamps
of the truck picked out the long low lines of a rambling
timber homestead with its sweep of lawns and
backdrop of lofty trees.

Lanie breathed a sigh of relief. So they were
approaching civilisation at last! Her apprehensions fell
away and her spirits lifted on a wave of anticipation.
Remote, lonely, the place might be, but all the same the
new job sounded definitely exciting! She was glad now
that she had taken this position as cook in the outback,
even if it entailed having Jard as her boss. One thing
was for sure, her soft lips quirked at the thought, he
wouldn't be likely to seek her company any more than
was strictly necessary.

'Look like there's a power failure again!' Jard's
laconic tones cut across her musing.

'Breakdown somewhere,' Sandy agreed. Neither man
appeared to be particularly concerned at the power

failure. Maybe, Lanie thought, they were used to such inconveniences.

They were sweeping into a wide concrete driveway and Jard was braking to a stop at the flight of steps approaching the verandah that appeared to run around three sides of the big old house. Certainly, the big rambling house was no cottage, Lanie thought, puzzled, but maybe they were calling in here for some reason. She was still trying to fathom the mystery as Jard got out and moving around the vehicle, flung open the door. Sandy and Lanie dropped to the ground. The next minute Jard had reached into the truck for her travel bag and soon she found herself walking up the long flight of steps with the two men.

The thoughts flew chaotically through her mind. Had Sandy actually mentioned that dream cottage or was that a figment of her imagination? She couldn't be certain. She would have a small family to cook for. Sandy and his son Jard lived in the outback. That she knew to be the information she had been given. But the cottage . . . Well, she would soon find out the truth of the matter. So she went on up the steps, conscious of the intense silence of the country and the brilliance of the stars—a spangled embroidery on the dark blue velvet of the night sky.

As they reached the creeper-hung porch, a door opened and a girl came hurrying towards them. Or rather, Lanie realised the next moment, she hurried towards Jard. Even in the gleam of a hanging lantern Lanie could see that the girl was quite lovely to look at—dark, sleek, sophisticated.

'Welcome home, darling!' The girl ran to Jard and raising herself on tiptoe, kissed him on the cheek. '*Gorgeous* to see you!' Her voice came from somewhere in the region of her chest. 'I thought you were never coming! Then I got the jitters and I got to thinking you'd had a smash on the road!'

'Oh, come on, honey,' Jard's tone was indulgent as gently he disengaged the clinging arms from around his neck. 'You know me better than that!'

'And you didn't even find a cook, after all that time?' She eyed him laughingly.

It was Sandy who answered. 'We did, you know.'

But the stranger, her eyes still fixed on Jard's face, didn't seem to be listening. 'But what took you so long?'

'We had a breakdown, among other things.' Sandy's tone was oddly cool and the thought flashed through Lanie's mind that the dark girl's beauty and imperious manner (funny how the two attributes so often went together) held no particular attraction for the older man.

'Paula,' Lanie realised Jard was speaking, his tone expressionless, 'this is Lanie. We brought her back with us from town.'

'Hi.' The other girl acknowledged the introduction with the barest inclination of her dark head. She scarcely glanced towards Lanie, hidden in the shadows of the long dimly-lighted hallway.

'Paula happens to be our nearest neighbour,' Sandy explained as the group moved on down the candlelit passage.

'That's me!' Paula had hooked her arm affectionately through Jard's. 'I'm always driving the odd twenty miles over here for advice from Jard. When it comes to expert advice about training a show jumper or breeding or buying horses, I just couldn't get along without him.' Her gaze returned to his face. 'I waited and waited, hoping you'd turn up, and in the end I decided to stay the night. I guess now,' she pouted, 'it's too late and I'll have to wait for morning. You see, Jard, I couldn't wait to tell you, I've got this young show jumper on a week's trial and I just had to ask your opinion of it.'

Lanie was only half aware of the strong tones. For they had reached a comfortable-looking, spacious room with worn rugs lying on a polished floor. Flames crackled and soared in a great stone fireplace and the mellow glow of candles fell softly over walls hung with family portraits and pictures of horses and riders. Lanie took in the hand-crafted furniture, the deep restful leather-covered chairs, crimson velvet curtains pulled across french doors. It was all a far cry from the setting she had envisaged. She brought her mind back to Paula's assertive tones. 'I thought you might know this horse by name——' Her voice trailed away. For the first time she looked directly towards Lanie, her gaze taking in the sweetly curved mouth and blunt, freckled nose, the petite figure and round dimpled face.

'Jard said he brought you from town, but he didn't elaborate.' Paula's eyes held an expression of avid interest. 'Just a holiday, is it?' she prompted.

'Not really.' Lanie flung a glance towards Jard, but of course he was no help to her at all. She could see that the brute was positively enjoying her discomfiture. The knowledge sparked her to say defiantly, 'Seems they were looking for someone to help out with the cooking here for a while——'

'Cooking?' Paula broke into peals of laughter. She had a hateful laugh, Lane thought, loud and strident, and the matter wasn't even funny. 'You did say that you'd engaged a cook——?' Her incredulous gaze moved from Jard's closed face to Lanie.

'That's right,' Sandy cut in. 'Lanie turned out to be just what we were looking for.' Clearly enchanted with her youth and freshness, he added warmly, 'And pretty too!'

Paula was a pretty girl herself, Lanie thought, with her suntanned skin and shiny hair. Or would be, if it weren't for the angry twist of her small mouth and the resentment that smouldered in the dark eyes. If it were Jard who was on her mind, Lanie could have told her she had no need to worry on her account—on the contrary!

'We're darned grateful to her,' Sandy was saying, 'for coming to help us out in the cooking department while Edna's off enjoying herself overseas.'

Paula shrugged her shoulders. 'I guess Jard had to take whatever the agency for domestic workers had got on their books—and put up with the consequences!' She turned away as though the matter of Lanie's arrival here was a matter of no further interest to anyone.

Lanie felt the blood rising to her cheeks. Of all the nerve! She didn't have to endure this sort of treatment from a strange girl. She opened her mouth in a sharp retort, and only Sandy's restraining touch on her arm stopped the indignant words that trembled on her lips.

'Lanie's a top-notcher with the cookbook,' Sandy said smoothly. 'Would you believe, she's just won a national flour promotion cooking contest!'

Oh dear. Lanie's chagrin was replaced by a feeling of frustration. Sandy's warm championship of her kitcheneering talents had only served to make matters worse, for how could she possibly live up to such glowing recommendations?

'I'm not really all that good,' she protested in her soft husky tones, but no one appeared to be listening to her. Or maybe, she thought on a sigh, they didn't believe her. All the time she was uneasily aware of Jard's gaze fixed on her face and she just knew he'd be wearing that hateful mocking expression. He was. Hastily she averted her glance.

'I'm glad she's going to come to the rescue.' Sandy had moved to her side, and she had the ridiculous thought that he seemed in some way to be protecting her.

'Actually,' Paula's strong tones rang out, 'I'll have you all know that *I'm* the one who's helping you out right now!' She flashed a brilliant smile in Jard's direction. 'I've put on a meal for you! I know what you are, Jard, for skipping meals once you get on the road. With you it's all go! I've got it ready,' she indicated a pottery casserole standing on bricks close to the blazing fire. 'The power didn't cut out until I had everything cooked, so I lit the fire to keep the food warm. Better make the most of a good meal, Jard, now that you've taken on a new cook—you know something?' Suddenly she had flung around to face Lanie. 'I just can't believe you haven't been stringing a line to Jard and Sandy to get yourself a job.' The dark eyes were bright with malice. 'I saw that flour promotion contest advertised in the newspapers and you didn't have to cook a thing, all you had to do was to send in a bread recipe. Admit it, now!'

'I know, but——'

'What a joke!' Once again Paula broke into laughter.

Well, if that was the way she wanted it, Lanie thought hotly, she would give the other girl something to laugh about. 'That's right. Sandy——'

'Sandy? Already?' Paula raised her brows in simulated surprise. 'Did you hear that, Jard?'

Lanie's cheeks were pink, but she wasn't beaten yet. 'Sandy offered to bring my electric range with me.' She added airily, 'I thought I might as well use my prize cooker.' At least, she thought with some satisfaction, she had put a stop to Paula's peals of laughter. How could such an attactive-looking girl have so harsh a voice? she wondered.

'Your—what?' Paula was gazing towards Lanie incredulously. The next moment she appeared to pull herself together. 'That won't be much use to you when the power goes off, like it did tonight! It was just lucky for everyone that I happened to be here to put on a meal for them on the open fire.'

Everyone, Lanie queried inwardly, or Jard? Oh well, it was really no concern of hers. It seemed to Lanie that the other girl couldn't take her gaze from Jard's face. No wonder he's so arrogant, she mused, if this is the way girls treat him in his little neck of the woods. Hanging on to his every word with rapt attention. But not this girl!

He was taking no part in the conversation as he stood at the sideboard, riffling through a pile of envelopes propped up on the shelf. All at once he glanced up from his correspondence to eye Paula enquiringly. 'Where's Clara got to tonight?' His tone sharpened. 'She's not ill, is she?'

Clara? Lanie was fitting the puzzle together. Wasn't she the housekeeper Sandy had told her about? Her thoughts were in turmoil. So this must indeed be Jard's home.

Paula shrugged her shoulders. 'Don't ask me! I

don't know what she's so uptight about. She says she has a headache, but I think she's just sulking in her room. Wouldn't you think she'd be grateful to me for helping out here tonight?' Moving towards the leaping flames, she lifted the lid of a casserole standing on the bricks at the side of the hearth. 'Instead of getting up on her high horse and taking herself off to her room— Not,' she flashed Jard a brilliant smile, 'that it makes much difference whether she's here or not. What she does around the place is negligible.' She turned a face flushed with the flames. 'Ready when you are, Jard!'

'Sorry, girl.' Lanie became aware of Sandy's contrite tones. He had picked up her travel bag. 'Afraid I'm not much of a host. I'll show you to your rooms and you can have a quick brush-up before dinner.' He guided her through a door and out into the darkness of a long passage. 'Your quarters are a bit away from the main part of the house. Edna likes it that way. She's left all her things just as they were, but that shouldn't worry you too much.' They moved through a back door and out into the starshine of the moonless night, then they crossed a grassy strip and approached a low timber dwelling. They climbed two steps, then Sandy flung open a door. 'Wait here a minute——' He strode ahead of her into the room, then struck a match and put a light to a candle on the dressing table. Even in the dimness Lanie realised it was a room of spartan simplicity, simply furnished, and smelling faintly of furniture polish. Beneath her feet she felt the softness of sheepskin rugs as she moved to the bed with its white cover, where Sandy had tossed down her travel bag.

'Bathroom's next door,' he told her cheerfully, 'with a toilet and shower, so you'll be quite self-contained. A word of warning, though——' She caught the teasing note in his voice.

'Goodness, what is it?'

'Part of Edna's decor arrangements. You'll find out soon enough. Just don't let it influence you too much while you're here! Edna's got a one-track mind when it comes to decorations.'

Lanie said, puzzled, 'I don't see——'

He chuckled. 'You will, come daylight. I'll put a candle in the bathroom and call back for you in ten minutes to see you to the house. How does that suit you?'

'But it's only a step——'

'It's flaming dark for a newcomer! Pick you up soon!' His genial tones drifted back to her as he turned away.

'Sandy!' She hurried after him. 'Wait—there's something I want to ask you about——'

'Not to worry, lass, we'll sort it out later!' She heard the closing of the door, then he had vanished into the night.

Left alone, Lanie stood looking around her. The candlelight threw fitful shadows over the big room with its old-fashioned dressing table and bed and huge wardrobe standing in a corner of the room. When the power came on again she would really be able to take in her surroundings. Meantime she was intrigued by Sandy's reference to a special feature of the room. It all appeared to be perfectly ordinary to her. Picking up the candlestick, she raised it high, then her lips quirked in amusement. For all around the walls were hung framed photographs of brides and wedding groups in styles and fashions that varied from many years previously up to the present day. Had Edna brought up a large family, she wondered, and all of the marrying kind? Suddenly she remembered Sandy's promise to call back for her. Golly, she would need to hurry!

The bathroom next door she found to be unexpectedly attractive with its marbled green shower, bath and basin and cream sheepskin rugs on the polished timber of the floor. She had a quick wash and ran a comb through her hair. Flame-coloured tendrils escaped from her topknot, but she couldn't be worried about the matter right now. Back in the bedroom she unzipped her travel bag. It was the work of only a few minutes to pull over her head a dark cotton knit top and to tie around her slim waist a wrap-around peasant skirt in soft amber tonings. At least, she mused, the change of garments had made her feel fresher, and anyway, who in the house would care about her appearance tonight, except maybe Sandy.

Paula cares. The thought came unbidden and she brushed it aside. To the other girl she was a nobody, scarcely worth a second glance. Well, that suited her. She had enough problems on her mind at the moment without worrying about Paula.

When Sandy escorted her back to the spacious dining room a little while later, Lanie realised that the gleaming polished wood of the long table at the end of the room was set with silver cutlery and firelight struck shafts of light in cut crystal goblets. For a makeshift meal, she mused, Paula appeared to have gone to a lot of trouble. All at once she became aware of a big man who appeared to be in his early forties who had risen from a deep chair to greet her. 'Lanie,' Sandy was saying, 'meet Mike, he's our head shepherd.'

She smiled up at the shy, pleasant face of the stranger, then immediately her glance slid away to Jard. She couldn't seem to help it. He was standing at the cocktail cabinet mixing drinks, his thatch of thick corn-coloured hair falling over a sun-bronzed forehead.

'For you, Paula. You deserve this for all your trouble tonight.' With a dazzling smile Paula accepted the glass he handed to her.

'What'll you have—Lanie?' She caught the cool note in his tone, the way he said her name as if it hurt him to pronounce it. He could scarcely ignore her, she reflected crossly, but having her here tonight gave him no joy, anyone could see that! Aloud she said quietly, 'Just a sherry, please.'

He crossed the room to hand her the goblet and once again she noticed the hard expression in his eyes.

Paula went to stand at his side, her gaze roving proudly over the firelit room and beautifully appointed table. 'Aren't you going to say it, Jard? Didn't she do *well*?'

The laughing, provocative face upturned to Jard, Lanie thought, was demanding attention, praise,

appreciation—or love? Now where had that thought
come from? These people were strangers to her, all of
them, except Sandy who in some odd fashion already
seemed to her to be someone she could trust, in spite of
his misleading information.

Could it be the firelight, she wondered, that lent
Jard's face that stern unrelenting look? His flat tones
gave nothing away. 'You sure saved our life.'

Paula's excited expression died away. Her eyes
dropped, the dark lashes veiling her expression. Had the
other girl expected a warmer welcome in view of all her
careful preparation tonight? Lanie wondered.

Around her the talk was becoming general, topics
that were as far removed from her own interests as
another world. The state of the stock markets, aerial
topdressing, the hill at the back of the station that was
due for a burn. There were discussions regarding
horses, mares and foals, mention of a blacksmith, a new
vet in the district. The long drive, the sherry, the
warmth of the firelit room combined to make her head
begin to buzz, but through it all one thing seemed clear.
Jard was the head of this small kingdom and they all
deferred to his judgment. Clearly the great white chief
was in command and rebellion of any sort would not be
tolerated. His warning, coolly delivered to her, echoed
in her mind with painful clarity. *'If you're going to work
for me, you'd better be good!'*

As she sipped her sherry she took in Jard's tall figure.
Even his stance was that of the man in command. There
was about him an autocratic air, his whole bearing that
of a man of substance and authority. Hadn't she felt the
force of his dominant personality from their moment of
meeting? Now at last she understood the reason. Not
that he appeared to throw his weight about, she had to
admit, watching his attentive expression as the head
shepherd reported to him on station matters during his
absence.

All at once she became aware that Sandy had
dropped down at her side on the deep settee. She turned
towards him impulsively. 'Tell me, Sandy. I had no idea

how things really were here. Jard owns this whole
property, doesn't he? He's a big runholder and this is
the station homestead—it must be!'

'Sure is, lass.'

'But why,' she cried exasperatedly, 'didn't you tell
me?'

Sandy's weathered, lined features puckered in a
rueful grin. 'Couldn't risk losing you, that's why! To be
truthful, there were certain personal reasons too, a little
plan of mine I'm hoping might come off——' He broke
off. 'But we won't go into that! Let's just say I had a
hunch that you'd fill the bill and what's more, you'd be
glad that you took the job down here!' His eyes were
twinkling in a leathery face. 'Even if I didn't go into too
many details about the acreage of Rangimarie!'

Lanie eyed him reprovingly, but she couldn't quite
subdue the glimmer of amusement in her eyes. 'How
many acres?'

'Five thousand odd, that's counting the hill country
at the back of the station—but don't let it throw you,'
his grin was warm and friendly, 'we're a small outfit
around here mealwise, except when the odd visitor
turns up.' Did she imagine the sudden hardening of his
tone? 'Like tonight! Why not look on your spell here as
a holiday?' He shot her a glance from those surprisingly
alert eyes, 'Right?'

A reluctant smile tugged at her lips. 'I guess so.' It
must be the effect of the sherry coursing through her
veins together with the warmth of the firelit room, she
decided, that was causing her to find the decision so
easy to make. Or could it be the challenge of the master
of Rangimarie? He was standing at the other end of the
room and she felt sure that he was deliberately ignoring
her, leaving Sandy the duty of entertaining her on this,
her first night at their home. That attitude of Jard's, she
promised herself, was something she was going to
change. Somehow she would *make* him notice her, and
what was more, come to recognise her as a worthwhile,
caring sort of girl despite her youth and inexperience
and the utterly mistaken opinion he appeared to have

formed regarding her. She would need to be on her
guard, though, for there was one thing, she admitted
reluctantly, that he did have, besides his wildly
attractive appearance. Never before had she encountered a man who projected such a powerful aura of
masculinity. What a triumph it would be to force him
to admit that he had been dead wrong in his snap
judgment of her capabilities. Turn her back on his job?
Go rushing back to town simply because conditions
here hadn't transpired to be those she had imagined?
Never!

'You know something?' she told Sandy. 'I'm going to
enjoy the experience!' But what she really meant was
teaching Jard a well-deserved lesson and not just the
matter of a different type of work and a fresh
environment.

Sandy let his breath on a long sigh of relief. 'That's
my girl!' The words fell into a pool of silence. 'It's a
deal! Shake on it!' The next moment she became aware
of Jard's watchful glance. Could it be the flickering
shadows of the flames, she wondered, that lent his face
that tight, angry expression? Surely he didn't imagine—
he couldn't—— On an impulse she snatched her soft
hand from Sandy's firm grasp. It was ridiculous, the
way she was letting Jard get under her skin!

A little later, seated beside Sandy at the long polished
table, Lanie felt glad of the older man's championship
tonight. Her gaze flickered over gleaming silverware
and the fine china of the dinner service that, like the
furniture in the room, she suspected to have been
brought out by sailing ship from England a century
earlier by a pioneer family who had sacrificed the
comforts of their life to hack a way through virgin bush
on the other side of the world.

As the meal proceeded she had to admit that Paula
wasn't, as the saying went, just a pretty face. The chilled
honeydew melon was delicious, the beef Wellington
perfectly cooked and the tamarillo dessert served with
rich dairy cream had a melt-in-the-mouth quality. The
silver candelabrum shed its mellow light over the wine

bottles, caught gleams in the table surface and made Paula look more beautiful than ever, Lanie thought. She really was attractive, she mused wistfully, with all the power that beauty gives a woman.

Jard, seated at the head of the table with Paula beside him, appeared to be entranced by Paula's conversation. The two seemed oblivious of both Sandy and Lanie, and once again Lanie formed the impression that Sandy wasn't enamoured of Paula's charms. Odd, she wondered how any man could feel that way—but then the other girl spared scarcely a glance for Jard's father. All her attention was given to the man at her side. If this was the way girls reacted to Jard's undeniable masculine magnetism, hanging on his every word, gazing up at him with rapt attention, then, Lanie decided once again, it was high time that he was taught a lesson.

When the meal came to an end, Mike bade the others goodnight and went out of the room. Lanie surmised that he was going back to his own quarters. Paula moved to the stereo and soon the pulsing beat of dance music flowed through the room. She threw Jard a meaningful, laughing look, tapping her foot in time with the rhythm, but he was standing by the sideboard once again, reading correspondence. A little at a loss as to what to do, Lanie began to stack the plates together. All at once she realised Paula had come to join her. 'I suppose you did have some references from the employment agency?' The other girl's strident tones were reduced to a whisper.

'I didn't come through the agency.' The next moment Lanie realised she had given herself away.

'Where on earth,' Paula asked sneeringly, 'did Jard find you, then?' The words implied, Lane thought hotly, that she had been scarcely worth the trouble of bringing here.

'It wasn't Jard.' Lanie's soft lips tightened. 'Sandy offered me the job.'

Paula's arched brows rose incredulously. 'Sandy?'

'That's right.' Lanie was clattering plates together. 'I

happened to meet up with him in town and he offered me the temporary work.'

'That's just like him. He'd fall for any soft touch. I suppose he was feeling sorry for you?'

Lanie, however, had had more than she could endure of this inquisition. 'I was sorry for *him*,' she flashed. 'He was stuck for domestic help here, so——' she threw the other girl a challenging glance, 'here I am!'

Paula's mouth twisted with the derisive expression Lanie was fast coming to know. 'You've never tried domestic work before, though, have you?' Her glance went to Lanie's soft hands. 'Office work would be more in your line.' All at once her tone was urgent and demanding. 'Tell me, why did you come here *really*?'

'Does it matter?' Lanie left her and moved towards Sandy, who was enjoying a pipe from his deep seat near the fire. 'The kitchen, please?' she enquired with a smile. 'Where is it?'

'Down the passage and first on the left—come along, I'll show you.' Picking up a candlestick from the dresser, he led the way.

'How long will the power cut last, do you think?' She carried a pile of plates in her arms as she followed him out of the room.

'Your guess is as good as mine. Could be an hour or two, could be all night. Here we are!' He flung open a door and stood looking around him for a place on which to set down the candlestick.

Lanie, peering over his shoulder, saw his difficulty only too well. For even in the dimness she discerned that dishes, pots and pans were flung haphazardly over every available surface. The kitchen looked modern enough, what she could see of it, for clearly Paula had concentrated her energies on her culinary efforts and left the cooking utensils to chance—and the new cook!

'Helluva mess around here,' Sandy said under his breath. 'No use trying to do anything about it tonight, lass, not in this light. Tell you what—I'll give you an early call in the morning. No need to put on breakfast until nine o'clock. You'll have swags of time to whack things into shape by then.'

Lanie gazed helplessly around her. 'But——'

'Okay, then,' he conceded, 'we'll take the things off the table and shove the dirty stuff in the sink, if there's any room. No use hoping Paula will do anything about this lot. She's not the sort to worry about things like that!'

Lanie was eyeing the yellow-painted room. A massive deep-freeze cabinet ran along one wall, there was a refrigerator, a stainless steel sink bench beneath the clutter of food-smeared crockery. 'Couldn't we just put away the foodstuffs?' she pleaded.

'If you really want to.' Together they carried out from the dining room milk, cream, sugar, cheese and biscuits. Sandy pushed it all out of sight in various cupboards. 'You can sort it all out in the morning!' he told her cheerfully. Lanie wished she felt as optimistic in the matter. Could this be the reason why the housekeeper had pleaded a headache? Lanie wondered. Really, one couldn't blame her!

Try as she would, Sandy was not to be budged from his edict. 'Easy to cope with in daylight,' he told her, 'but not tonight. You've had a long day. What you need now is a good night's sleep.'

'Well, if you say so. I think I'll slip away now.' Not, she reflected, that anyone would notice whether she was in the other room or not.

Long after she had got into bed she lay wakeful as the events of the long day chased one another through her mind. Maybe, she thought at last, if she read for a while she could settle down, banish from her thoughts Jard's compelling face with his set angry expression. It wasn't as if he *mattered*, yet deep down she knew that in some inexplicable way, he did!

Slowly the time crept on. She must have dozed off, for suddenly she awoke to a lighted room. Of course, she had left the switch of the bedside light turned on. Now the bridal pictures had sprung to life. Lanie couldn't help giggling to herself. There were so many brides, and all looking so fatuously pleased with themselves.

All at once she remembered the cluttered kitchen that would take her at least an hour to clean up and must be faced in the morning before she could even begin to get familiar with her surroundings. *But it needn't be in the morning.*

Swiftly she dropped her feet to the fluffy sheepskin rug beside the bed and pulled on her old white candlewick robe. Opening the door, she peered towards the homestead, but there seemed no glow of light in the back of the house where the kitchen was situated. And if she was ever so quiet . . . The next minute she was out of the door and running across the dew-wet grass on bare feet. Her hair flowed loosely around her shoulders but no matter. There would be no one to see her.

Cautiously she opened the kitchen door, closed it behind her and put a hand to the light switch. The scene that sprang into sight before her eyes was daunting. Stacks of plates balanced precariously on sink bench and table, there were pots and pans with congealed food stuck to the rims and everywhere dishes, dishes of all description. She couldn't decide where to make a start, then she pushed the sleeves of her robe above her elbows, emptied the sink of cold greasy water and turned on the hot tap. Before long she had piled plates and dishes on the draining rack and a portion of the long steel bench became visible. Absorbed in her task, she hadn't heard the opening of the door until a sound alerted her and she swung around to find herself staring straight into Jard's eyes.

In that second some unseen force tingled between them, powerful and breathtaking—at least it was to her. It was a moment or so before she could drag herself from the impact.

'So it's you again!' He was leaning against the door jamb, thumbs hooked in his low-slung leather belt, his tone deceptively indolent. How could it be, she wondered, that he contrived to give the impression that she was doing something wrong?

'That's right,' she said lightly, and muttered under her breath, 'You didn't really imagine that Paula would be working in here cleaning up the mess, did you?' She endeavoured to make her voice sound carefree. 'Just getting things cleared up ready for a good start in the morning!'

She was unaware of the bright cloud of hair tumbling over her white candlewick gown as she swung back to her task. 'I'll soon be finished.' Something in his narrow-eyed appraisal was disconcerting, very, and to escape his glance she nonchalantly wiped dry a dish for the second time.

'I was having a session with some book work in the office,' he was saying. 'I couldn't believe my ears when I heard someone clattering away down here at this hour in the morning.'

Heavens, she wondered wildly, what was the time? In her haste to get on with the job she hadn't even glanced at her watch in the bedroom. 'I've only got another half hour or so's work,' she murmured.

'That's where you're wrong,' he drawled, and even without glancing in his direction she was aware that he hadn't moved his position. 'Knock it off, Lanie. We're not slave-drivers around here!'

She didn't look around. 'If it's all the same to you——'

'It's not!'

'I want to tidy up here so that I won't waste any time in the morning. That is,' she added in a voice sparked with anger, 'if you want a cooked breakfast to come along on time!'

He came striding towards her, lips compressed and eyes dark with anger. 'Finish it tomorrow.'

She wielded a sponge mop furiously on a plate. 'No!'

'Listen to me!' The hidden anger and suspicion she had sensed in him throughout the day surfaced in his low, grated tone. Even without turning around she knew that he was furious with her for daring to disobey the boss's orders.

His tone was dangerously quiet. 'Do I have to carry you away?'

Lanie pushed the bright hair back from her forehead and turned a flushed, defiant face towards him. Why was she trembling? 'You just try!'

'Right—you've asked for it!'

She tensed herself, then suddenly relaxed as a masculine voice said suddenly, 'Hey, Lanie, what goes on? Kitchen staff don't work overtime around here!' Sandy stood behind Jard, peering into the room. He wore a dressing gown over pyjamas and had evidently been aroused from sleep, his bemused gaze taking in Lanie's eyes that sparkled with anger.

'Just what I've been trying to get through to her,' Jard said coolly, 'but she doesn't seem to be co-operating very well.'

Spiritedly Lanie splashed the dishes in the water in the sink, then had to wipe away drops of moisture from her eyes with the back of her hand. 'I'm only doing my job,' she said defiantly, 'and if I like to choose my own hours——'

'I see your point lass,' Sandy's voice was placating. 'Thing is, the way things are looking right now,' he swept a hand towards the neatly piled clean plates, 'you've got this lot pretty well licked into shape. Leave those cups to dry on the rack and you'll have a head start for breakfast. Better call it a day, girl!' His smile was really friendly, Lanie thought. He understood how she felt. He knew his son had been bullying her, or trying to. Thank heaven Sandy had arrived in the nick of time to save her from being bodily removed from the scene.

She flashed a smile in Sandy's direction. 'You know something? I just might take your advice!' Squeezing out the dishmop, she hung it over the sink and said in the most noncommittal voice she could summon up, 'I've got my bearings here now anyway.' Disconcertingly aware of Jard's glance, she turned away, 'I'll say goodnight, then.'

''Night, lass.'

Lanie would have liked to leave too, but Jard, so tall, so still, menacing almost, blocked her way. He was leaning against the door jamb, arms folded across his sinewy chest and a determined light in his grey eyes.

'I'll see you to the cottage,' he said gruffly, and she knew it was the last thing in the world he really wanted to do.

'Don't bother——' She made a rush, trying to dart beneath his arm, but he was too quick for her. Somehow Lanie knew it was just no use arguing with him, so she went with him in silence as they crossed the passage and went out of the back door.

Outside a full moon had risen high in the sky, silvering sloping lawns and throwing long shadows over the grass around them. Lanie, trying to hurry ahead of him, stumbled, and he put a hand on her elbow.

Angrily she flung away. 'I can manage!' Immediately she tripped over the edge of a pathway, and this time he kept a peremptory hold on her bare arm as he marched her towards the cottage. Once there he flung open the door and stepped inside. Putting a hand to the electric light switch, he flooded the room with light. Lanie was about to face him indignantly, but he had turned away. She barely caught his grated, ''Night', then he had vanished into the silver-shadowed world outside.

CHAPTER FOUR

LANIE wakened to the shrill peal of her alarm clock and for a few moments she lay dozing, vaguely aware of her unfamiliar surroundings. How come, she wondered hazily she was here in a room where each wall was decorated with pictures of wedding parties and bridal groups? Recollection came with a rush. *That man!* That arrogant, domineering—sensationally good-looking— she thrust the thought aside—owner of the place whom she had unwittingly acquired as her boss.

She dropped her feet to the sheepskin rug on the floor and running to the window, swept the floral curtains aside. As she took in the vista outspread before her she felt a mounting sense of excitement. Somehow, in spite of everything, and everything included the most infuriating man she had ever met in her life, she was glad she'd come.

Below the translucent blue of the sky, range after range of hills marched away to the horizon and in the distance rose the irregular, haunting cone of Egmont. Close at hand the bush-filled gullies formed natural divisions of sheep-threaded paddocks. So this was Rangimarie. No neighbours, no hint of the outside world. Her gaze shifted to a hill paddock where horses, tails raised and manes flying, streaked over green slopes. Further up the rise, black steers huddled together in a grove of cabbage trees. Above the lowing of cattle she caught the dull roar of the sea, and craning her head, she caught a glimpse of glinting black sand and a windswept coast where great waves hurled themselves against precipitous cliffs.

At that moment she caught the sound of a man's footfall on the path and a moment later Jard, whistling a tune, strolled away from the homestead. Her gaze followed the lean muscular figure, taking in the erect carriage and easy stride. If one didn't have first-hand knowledge of his horrible nature . . . It must be because of the antagonism he sparked in her that she couldn't seem to wrench her glance aside. She watched him until he reached the stables, where he was joined by the quiet-eyed head shepherd named Mike whom she had met last night, and two young stockmen. No doubt, she mused, Jard was giving the men their work directions for the day.

It was a luxury to possess her own bathroom, and after a quick shower she was back in her bedroom. Running a brush over her hair, she gathered up the shining strands and pinned them in a knot high on her head. She refused to give Jard the chance of accusing her of an unhygienic attitude towards her duties. No need for make-up today, for who ever heard of a glamorous station cook? Presently she was ready, in comfortable worn jeans and white cotton T-shirt, for her day's work. If only Paula didn't come to breakfast with the others.

The odd thing—she paused for a moment in her headlong rush—was that her mirrored reflection was that of a girl with shining eyes, her whole appearance that of someone who was filled with a sense of anticipation and excitement. Just as if she were about to take up the duties she had originally hoped for instead of working in the station kitchen and being treated as an intruder. At least that appeared to be Jard's attitude towards her. As if she cared! Tilting her rounded chin, she marched determinedly out of the room.

When she opened the door she stepped out into an invigorating new world where the air was unbelievably clear and fresh with the salt tang of the sea. Early morning sunshine streamed over the long verandahs running around three sides of the house and lightened the mellow red of the roof. In the light of day she saw that the rambling old *kauri* building, with rooms added haphazardly, could be a century old but kept in good repair. There was a backdrop of towering trees, and spacious lawns sloped away from the building.

Suddenly, as she approached the back entrance, she had the oddest feeling, almost as though she were coming home. Jard's home? She must be out of her skull!

In the gentle sunlight the kitchen appeared modern and convenient. Evidently, she thought, Jard had already made himself an early morning cuppa, for a used cup stood on the sink. She decided that while the chops were frying on the old-fashioned electric range, she would finish drying the dishes she had left last night, or was it this morning? She was reaching to a shelf for a pan when she looked around to see a slight, frail-looking little woman of middle age, who was standing in the doorway.

'Oh, hello!' The small woman had fair hair turning to grey, Lanie noticed, and a worried expression. 'You must be Clara?'

'That's right.' Clara had a singularly sweet smile, Lanie thought. Crossing the room, the older woman came to stand at the sink bench beside Lanie. 'Did Jard tell you that I'm his housekeeper——' She broke off, sending Lanie a puzzled glance. 'You're not, you couldn't be——'

'The new cook? I am, you know.' Lanie's lips quirked at the woman's disbelieving expression. 'Sandy and Jard brought me down from Auckland yesterday.'

'You look awfully young,' Clara murmured doubtfully, adding as if to herself, 'But I suppose the employment agency recommended you to Jard——'

'Well, actually——'

Clara, however, was not listening. 'I hope you're not going to try out a lot of those foreign concoctions on us,' she said reprovingly. 'Edna believes in serving good plain food.'

'Oh no, I'm not!' Lanie assured her. Well, she thought, that was true enough. Her meagre knowledge of the culinary arts wouldn't run to anything of a complicated nature. To change the subject she said, 'Paula told me you weren't well last night. Are you feeling better now?'

Clara's pale blue eyes shifted evasively. 'I wasn't all

that bad.' She drew herself up, her voice thick with emotion. 'I will not be dictated to by *that girl*! Just because she's known Jard for years and years she thinks she belongs here! She's not mistress at Rangimarie yet, for all her airs and graces and the way she orders me around——' She added with dignity, 'And me the housekeeper here. When my husband died and I was all alone in the world,' she ran on, 'and Jard offered me a home here I said, "I know I'm your aunt, but I won't come to stay with you indefinitely unless I can be of some use around the place." And Jard, he's so kind, said quick could be, "Right, Aunt Clara! As from now you're appointed official housekeeper of the homestead! Now will you come?" So of course that was different. I mean to say, one does have one's pride.'

'Of course.' Lanie, spooning fat into the hot pan, nodded. So her random guess had proved to be correct and this nervous little woman was one of the family here.

'All that fuss,' Clara had gathered up two crystal goblets from the table, 'trying to impress Jard with what a marvellous wife she'd make for him! If you ask me, she'd be wasting her time thinking she can take over here one of these days. Who does Paula think she is?' Lanie feared for the safety of the crystal goblets Clara banged on the table to emphasise her point. 'Even if she does have the looks to turn any man's head,' she added grudgingly, 'and knows how to make the most of herself!' After a moment she went on, 'She was brought up on a sheep farm not so far away from here and when her parents died she got a manager in to look after the place. Nowadays she uses her old home as a base, a sort of stopover between her overseas trips and moving around the country judging at horse shows and gymkhanas. I suppose,' she admitted reluctantly, 'it's only natural she'd want to spend most of her time over here.' Clara's small mouth tightened. 'But that doesn't give her the right to take over the household management when Edna's away.' Evidently, Lanie reflected, the memory of the superbly prepared meal

Paula had produced still rankled. 'I could have managed perfectly well,' Clara declared, 'without her interference.'

Lanie made soothing noises. 'I'm sure you could.' Inwardly she was wondering why Paula spent so much of her time here. The other girl's striking sppearance and supreme self-confidence was a combination that would surely draw masculine attention wherever she went. Surely Paula would have a choice of male companions.

But not of Jard's calibre. The answer came unbidden. A runholder with vast estates, a man of authority with heart-stopping good looks. And if that weren't sufficient to make any woman aware of him, he possessed that indefinable aura of masculinity— powerful, potent, irresistible. Why, even she could feel the impact, and she didn't even like the man! Lanie wished she could stop thinking about Jard. He was spoiling a perfectly good morning.

'Why does Jard ask her to come here?' The words seemed to come without her volition.

'Oh, Paula doesn't wait to be *asked*,' scoffed Clara. 'She just arrives here in between her overseas trips buying new show jumpers or collecting trophies at horse events over in England. Oh, she always has some perfectly plausible excuse for coming here. Usually it's a horse she has got on trial and she needs Jard's advice about it. Wouldn't you think that a woman who spends half her time travelling and buying and selling show jumpers would be able to make up her own mind? Sometimes I wonder that Jard doesn't get sick and tired of having her around all the time.'

Lanie couldn't help the thought that he didn't appear at all reluctant to entertain Paula, and there seemed little doubt but that she was making a play for Jard. Really, she mused, it served him right, and she wondered why the thought was so depressing.

She wrenched her mind back to Clara's tones. 'Mind you,' she was saying reluctantly, 'Paula could feel she has some claim on Jard because of Dell——'

Lanie despised herself for listening to gossip, but somehow she just had to know the rest of the story. She glanced across at Clara enquiringly. 'Dell?' Lanie found she was holding her breath for the answer.

'Paula's older sister. Now she was the one Jard was really crazy about. I never saw him look so happy as in those days when he and Dell had their wedding plans made and everything to look forward to.' Clara's face sobered. 'Then she was killed one wet night when the car she was driving missed the bridge and went into the river. That was three years ago, and Jard hasn't been the same man since. He doesn't laugh so easily somehow and he seems to bury himself in his work.' Clara seemed to tune in on Lanie's unspoken question. 'Not that the girls don't like him a lot, especially Paula, but he just doesn't seem interested. Dell was so different from Paula, quiet and thoughtful with a lovely low speaking voice—— My goodness! Here they are!'

Lanie had caught the echo of male voices from outside the open window and a moment later the tread of heavy boots sounded on the path approaching the house. A frenzied glance at the chops, so much more massive than any she had previously had to contend with, told her they were not yet ready.

'Don't worry,' Clara told her, 'they'll take a while to scrub up out on the porch.' She carried away the last of the silverware and crystal. 'Breakfast is in here. I'll set the table for you.'

'Oh, would you?' Lanie hurried back to the electric range.

By the time Jard and Sandy came into the kitchen, she had prepared glasses of orange juice and had placed hot plates down on the table. She was proud of the heated plates. She really had thought of everything, she congratulated herself.

'Morning, Lanie!' Sandy, wearing khaki drill shorts and short-sleeved cotton shirt, looked infinitely more at home, she thought, than in his city suit.

'Morning!' She smiled across at him, slipping the sizzling meat on to plates. Jard sent her a brief nod.

What had she expected of him? She busied herself placing slices of hot toast in the rack and pouring out tea. She had to ask him, 'How do you like your tea?'

'As it comes.' If only he wouldn't watch her so intently, she thought distractedly, she would be more in control of her emotions. Just the knowledge of his nearness was making her feel flustered. She pushed the cup across the table to him, slopping tea in the saucer, and out of a corner of her eye she was aware of his satirical glance. The next moment as he cut into the meat she saw with horror that the chop was cooked only on the surface. Those monstrous chops would never cook properly, she thought wildly. His raised eyebrows and the mocking gleam in his eyes did nothing to ease her chagrin.

The next minute Sandy had swooped on the meat, tossing it back in the pan. 'Give them another few minutes, lass. Guess you're used to city chops. The real thing takes a little longer to cook.' Grinning, he eyed his son. 'Eh, Jard?'

'True.' Jard's tone was noncommittal. He had opened a newspaper and had apparently lost all interest in her cooking activities, Lanie thought. Somehow, though, she was hotly aware of his silent triumph. 'You *say* you're a cook——' Why must his scathing words return at this moment to her mind to flick her anew? Viciously she picked up a fork and jabbed at the slow-slow cooking meat. The fat splashed upwards and in a flash Sandy was at her side. 'That didn't hit you in the eye, did it?'

'No, no.' Scarlet-faced, hot, angry, she turned aside to escape Jard's gaze. What was it about him that reduced her nerves to shreds? She wiped the spot from her forehead with the back of her hand and tried to concentrate on the frying pan. At last, just when she had despaired of the meat ever being cooked, the chops were ready, and to her relief both men left clean plates.

'No breakfast for you?' Sandy asked her, but Lanie shook her head.

'I'll fix something for myself later.'

'Yuk—hogget chops again—don't cook any for me!' Paula, in her sea-green satin nightdress and matching negligee, had come into the room. Ignoring Sandy and Lanie, she went to Jard and leaned over his shoulder. 'Morning! Tell me, when can I get you to myself to give my new mare the once-over? It wouldn't take you long, and no one else could really tell me whether she's worth keeping or not.'

He glanced up and Lanie saw that there was no particular emotion in his direct gaze. 'Give me an hour. I've got to take a run down to the woolshed for a starter.'

'Lovely. See you then.' Paula poured herself tea, then drifted away, her cup in her hand. The next moment Lanie caught Clara's sibiliant whisper. 'It will take her that long to put on her make-up,' she said waspishly. But Lanie couldn't help the thought that Paula, with or without make-up, was a vision of loveliness that surely no man could resist. Except Jard, of course, who appeared impervious to her charms. Or could it be that his outward demeanour was just a cover to mask his real feelings? And what on earth was his love life to do with her anyway?

It seemed to Lanie an age before the meal was over, and though she busied herself at the sink she was uneasily *aware* of Jard's presence. At least, she comforted herself, he didn't seem to want her to attend to his needs but helped himself to a second cup of tea and placed a slice of bread in the toaster.

He was moving towards the door when Sandy's pleasant tones arrested him. 'Wait! If you're heading down to the woolshed, how about taking Lanie with you for a spin? She doesn't know a thing about what's outside yet——'

'It's all right,' Lanie interposed in her soft husky tones. 'I want to get things straight here first. Later on I'll take myself for a stroll around and get my bearings.'

'A stroll around here could turn into a marathon,' Sandy joked. He flung Jard a grin. 'He can't wait to give you a rundown on what goes on around here, show you around——'

'No! Please!' In her agitation she grabbed at the plate that had slipped from her hand, but it fell to the floor, shattering into pieces. She bent down to collect the fragments. 'I've got a lot to do.' Determination lent an edge to her tone. 'Things I can't leave.'

'Oh, come on,' Jard's drawling voice sent alarm signals flying along her nerves. 'They can wait. A burn down to the woolshed could be quite an experience for a city girl like you. You might enjoy the ride!'

Still flushed from the heat of the range, she eyed him suspiciously. His unexpected offer covered some ulterior motive to put her down, she felt sure.

Clara, with well-meant intentions, ranged herself on the side of the enemy. 'You run along with Jard, Lanie. I'll clear up here.' What could she do?

Lanie sent Jard a glance from under her eyelashes. 'You don't have to run me around——'

All at once he was smiling, a smile she didn't trust one little bit. 'No trouble . . . a pleasure.'

There was nothing for it but to go with him out to the waiting Land Rover. He helped her up the high step, then went around the vehicle and slid in behind the wheel. 'Sandy tells me you're nuts about the country.' He put a hand to the starter and they swept around the drive and rattled over the cattlestop. 'That's why you took the position here, *he says*.'

Her clear gaze swept up to the closed masculine face. There it was again, the tightly set jaw and cold expression.

'It's true,' she breathed,' and I don't care,' she cried hotly, 'whether you believe me or not!'

'Oh, I believe you.' His tone was deceptively bland. 'And that was your only reason for coming?'

'Yes, it was!' she snapped.

'Right!' He was back to his hard, arrogant self. 'Hope you're not nervous about heights and all that?'

'Not a bit.' What did he mean? she wondered on a wave of apprehension. She wouldn't put it past him to put her through a hair-raising drive just for his own selfish reasons, to try to get rid of her by scaring the wits out of her.

At first it wasn't so bad. They sped along the curving track in the direction of a cluster of buildings ahead. There were stables, implement sheds and garages, and she could see pastureland dropping steeply down to the sea.

'Here we go!' All at once Jard made a sharp turn and they ran over a grassy patch towards a bank ahead. A bank? It was a sheer cliff, she realised a few moments later as they hurtled over the edge and plunged down the precipitous slopes. Jolted wildly from one side of the seat to the other, she made no demur. She couldn't anyway, she thought grimly, for all her energies were taken up with striving to keep her balance. To Lanie it seemed that the incline dropped down for ever as, buffeted and shaken, they lurched on. Dimly she was conscious of a jumbled picture of black sandhills and blue sea spinning dizzily before her eyes as they bumped over ledges in the cliff face. Without conscious thought she reached out to grip the nearest support, which happened to be Jard's sinewy brown arm. It was some time before she realised she was hanging on tightly to him and immediately she released her grip. Bumps, bruises, anything was preferable to being dependent on him for assistance.

At last, just when she had decided she couldn't endure one more moment of being thrown around, they lurched down on to a stretch of grass below the sandhills. Not a word from him about the hair-raising drive he had just put her through, she thought crossly, and if he imagined she was going to give him the satisfaction of complaining about it, he was very much mistaken. Soon they were driving past tall *karaka* trees and approaching a great timber woolshed with its ramp and holding pens.

Jard braked to a stop at the foot of a flight of steps leading up to the shearing shed and dropping to the ground, flung open the passenger door. He eyed her with his cool glance. 'Care to take a look around in the shed? I don't suppose you've ever been inside a shearing shed before?'

Was he throwing off at her, a city girl? Lanie wondered. Probably he was. Aloud she forced her voice to a light, enthusiastic note. 'Love to!'

Presently he was flinging open the door of the shed and Lanie climbed over the high step.

They moved into the shadowy interior over a floor slippery with the oil of a myriad fleeces, and Lanie, looking around her, took in the presses, tables and sorting benches. High above, the rafters were festooned with cobwebs and the windows, she thought, looked as though they had never ever been cleaned.

Jard had paused, his gaze scanning the scene around them, and she followed his glance. 'Just wanted to check that everything's okay for the shearers,' he tossed off.

Lanie's mouth fell open. 'Sh-shearers?' She could have kicked herself for that betraying stammer. A town girl she might be, but she had lived long enough in the country to know only too well that the visit of the shearing team meant to a farmer's wife the preparation of colossal meals and morning and afternoon smokos— all served bang on time, for the men were paid by the hour for their back-breaking toil in the blistering heat of the shed. And guess who, she had a hollow feeling in her midriff, would be the one called upon to produce the supplies of food! Aloud she asked, 'When—are they due to arrive?'

'Tomorrow morning, actually. I've jacked it all up with a local team—why are you looking at me like that?'

The beast! The hateful sadistic brute! He was enjoying her horrified reaction to his words, she could tell by the triumphant glimmer in his eyes. He'd scored a point over her, damn him, and was delighted with his victory.

'I've got news for you!' Through horror and confusion, she tried to gather her wits together. It was the glint of amusement in his grey eyes that sparked her to real anger. 'A bit more than you bargained for when you took on the job, hmm? But Sandy did tell you that we ran sheep as well as cattle down here?'

'Yes, but——' Suddenly the rage building up inside her spilled over. Jard's sardonic expression was just too much to bear. She looked up at him, eyes sparkling, a betraying flush mounting on delicate cheekbones. 'You arranged it specially, didn't you?' she flung at him. 'That phone call you put through from the motel yesterday——'

'No, I didn't!' At the fury in his expression she knew a moment of real fear that she had gone too far with this man who was, after all, a stranger to her. After a moment's silence he seemed to get control of himself, but she knew the anger was still there. Oh, it was there all right, in his low controlled tone. 'Don't flatter yourself!' he grated harshly. 'Do you really imagine that I run this station to suit the personal wishes of me or my staff? *Do you?*' His hard grey glance pierced her and Lanie couldn't sustain his look.

'No,' she admitted, 'but——'

'But you still think so? Let me put you right. If you're going to work on a station you may as well get it into that pretty head of yours——' Lanie got such a shock at the word 'pretty' that she glanced up at him quickly, but apparently he hadn't even noticed his slip of the tongue. She wrenched her mind back to the low tone, throbbing with anger. 'The main shearing's over. We shear twice a year down here. That way we can cope with the dirt and dust that otherwise can put us out of the market for carpet manufacturing of the wool. Last clip there were a few sheep that missed out, a couple of days' work for the shearing gang. Mike arranged for the team to be here in the morning.'

'I get it.' In spite of her earlier suspicions Lanie believed what had been said to be the truth. 'It's just bad luck for me, then.' She spoke her thoughts aloud.

'Not for an experienced cook!'

'I didn't say I was——' she flung at him hotly.

'In that case,' he returned smoothly, 'this is your big

chance, then. Put it that way.'

'Starting at seven in the morning, I suppose?' She was dismayed at the note of desperation in her tone. Why couldn't she toss the whole thing off with confidence, as Paula no doubt would have done in the same circumstances?

'Relax!' Jard was actually grinning down at her, even if it wasn't a really warm friendly sort of grin. 'This gang are Maoris who live around the district. I've offered to put them up in the shearers' quarters, but they prefer to sleep in their own homes and do the two hours' stint each way every day.'

'So?' This time Lanie managed to sound not quite so pathetic and hopeless.

'So there's no breakfast for you to worry about. Ten o'clock smoko, of course, you can rustle up some scones and sandwiches for that. Get one of the boys to run you down to the shed.'

Just like that, she thought bitterly.

'Lunch won't be too bad for you,' he was saying, just as if it were all a nothing thing, as no doubt it was to him. 'Pizza pies, cold salads, cold meat, that sort of stuff.'

The unfeeling brute! she thought, tight-lipped. If it weren't that he was so good-looking she really would hate him. As it was . . . she wrenched her mind back to the deep vibrant tones. 'Dinners are straightforward fare. Hot joints with roast potatoes and vegies, cold fruit, there's swags of ice cream in the freezer. Edna always gives them apple pies that they seem to appreciate a lot.'

I can't cope with this. The frantic thoughts were running through Lanie's mind. Then she caught the mocking expression in Jard's grey eyes. She couldn't cope, but she had to, she thought distractedly, if only to prove him wrong! Somehow, somehow, she would succeed in providing those vast quantities of food. And heaven help the shearers!

All at once she became aware that he was regarding her narrowly. 'Is it on?'

She drew a deep breath, raised her chin and tried to infuse an uncaring note into her voice. 'Why not?' The expression of surprise in Jard's suntanned face was gratifying. What had he expected of her? she wondered. That she would give up in despair and leave the station here and now? Was that what he wanted? Unconciously she sighed. There couldn't be much doubt on that point.

At that moment she was conscious of the stillness in the interior of the great room that stretched away into the shadows. A sort of waiting stillness. For no reason at all her heartbeats quickened.

'You surprise me!'

She raised her glance to his and once again something powerful, intangible, held their gaze enmeshed as a life force flashed its potent magic between them. The next moment he bent down to kiss her full on the lips. Now her heartbeats were really thudding. It was an effort to speak at all, let alone with any degree of composure. 'What,' she asked breathlessly, 'was that for?'

'Just sealing a bargain,' came the cool tones. 'Let's go, shall we?' He had flung around, and wordlessly Lanie went with him out into the sunshine. She was still feeling bemused by his kiss, which evidently had been to him a mere gesture. It must be the heady excitement of having accepted his challenge, she mused, that had awakened in her this feeling of radiant happiness and a heightened sense of perception. For never before had she seen a sky of such a dazzling blue or sunshine so bright that it sparked a myriad diamond flashes in the dark metallic sands.

When she had climbed back in the Land Rover Jard lowered his powerful muscular frame into the driver's seat and swung the vehicle around on the dried grass. Then they shot along a road beside the sea.

'It's got quite a history, Rangimarie,' he told her. 'In the early days this used to be the access road to the station. Everything they needed in the place had to come by boat. That was before the road was cut through the hills. They must have had fun and games in the old days, getting the bales of wool loaded into surfboats.'

'Especially in this wild sea.' Her gaze swept the bleached logs piled up on black sandhills, the white rolling surf. Inwardly, the thoughts raced through her mind. How odd that he's talking to me just as though I were any ordinary guest in his home. He must have forgotten who I *really* am. She stole a glance towards his strong profile, but his expression gave nothing away.

All at once she realised they were swinging into a wide sandy track curving up cleared, sheep-threaded slopes. To think, she reflected indignantly, that we could have taken this route down to the shearing shed—but instead Jard had chosen to put her through some sort of endurance test in the hairy drop down the cliff face. The physical discomfort she was still feeling sparked her to say spiritedly, 'This is the road down to the shed, isn't it? Why ever didn't you——'

'Take the easy way?' He threw her a satirical grin. 'Thought you might like the experience.'

'You could have asked me,' she muttered crossly.

'You'd have said no, and missed out on something good!'

'Like a bone-shaking ride I could well do without?'

'But I got the idea you liked the outback?' His tone was deceptively gentle. 'That that was what you wanted, to try out a new life in the country. Or did I read Sandy wrong about that?'

He had trapped her neatly, and to change the subject she said quickly, 'The shearing gang—I was wondering how long they'll be here.'

'Not long. A couple of days, that's all.'

A couple of days, she thought bleakly. To her it would be an eternity.

'All good experience,' he taunted her.

Lanie threw him an exasperated glance. 'Thanks very much!'

They turned into the main drive approaching the homestead and presently Jard braked to a stop below the sun-splashed verandah. 'I'll leave you here.'

She dropped down from the high step, throwing a muffled 'Thanks' over her shoulder. It was an effort to force herself to say the word, considering—well, everything. Maddening to find herself so shaken by his kiss. The thoughts flew through her mind as she went up the steps. What had impelled him? An impulse born of the intimacy of the shadowy shed and the company of a pretty girl? Well, he had told her she was pretty, even though he had made the observation in an offputting sort of way. A heart-knocking thought shot through her. Could it be that despite his unflattering, readymade opinion of her, he was attracted to her just a little, just for a moment, but all the same—— How about you? a voice asked deep in her mind, but hurrying up the steps, she avoided the answer to that one.

She was moving down the long carpeted hall when Paula's strong tones arrested her. 'Oh, there you are, Lanie!' Paula was standing at the door of the lounge room and Lanie realised with surprise that the other girl's glance lacked the suspicion and malice of the previous evening. 'There's someone waiting to see you,' she said.

'Me?' Lanie paused. 'But that's just not possible——'

'Anything's possible when you're in love with someone.' Paula's voice was almost friendly. 'That's what your friend Trevor told me!'

CHAPTER FIVE

TREVOR here! Lanie's spirits plummeted and the thoughts churned wildly through her mind. He had lost no time in following her to her new address—but then she had always known him to be a type of man who valued a possession or a friendship only when it went out of his reach.

'Well,' prompted Paula with her twisted smile, 'aren't you going to give him a welcome kiss? The poor guy's driven all night so as to get here quickly and he's been waiting for you here for ages. If that isn't love——'

Reluctantly Lanie followed Paula into the room.

'Here she is!' Paula sent him a dazzling smile, but Trevor had sprung from a deep chair and was hurrying towards Lanie, a solidly built young man wearing an impeccably cut city suit. Who else but Trevor, Lanie thought, would arrive looking perfectly turned out after an all-night car journey?

'Hi, sweetheart!' Never before had she seen his set features alight with excitement. 'I thought you were never coming!'

'Hello, Trevor.' Swiftly she turned her face aside to evade his kiss. She ran the tip of her tongue over dry lips. 'I didn't expect to see you again.' Why couldn't he accept what she had already made clear to him, that their unexciting relationship was finished for ever?

She realised that Paula, eyes glittering, was glancing curiously from Trevor to herself. Clearly the other girl had every intention of remaining in the room, taking in the conversation with avid interest. 'I'll make coffee,' Lanie said abruptly, and fled.

In the kitchen she plugged in the electric jug and soon, with hands that shook in spite of herself, she mixed instant coffee into pottery mugs and placed them on a tray.

When she got back to the sunlit room, Paula was all smiles. 'Trevor's been telling me all about you two. An office romance? I didn't think those things ever really happened, but it seems they do. A real romance, evidently. Aren't you lucky, Lanie, to have such a devoted fiancé? Following you all the way from Auckland!'

Lanie set down the tray with a bang. Her angry glance went to Trevor and he met her gaze unwaveringly. How she could have wasted so many months of her life in the company of this smug, self-opinionated man she would never know. Even now it was clear that he had no intention of taking her refusal to see him again seriously. Or pretending that he didn't.

'I've been telling Paula,' he took the steaming mug she handed to him, and went on in his dogmatic tones, 'about our plans for the future.' Was he trying to convince himself, she wondered, that everything between them was as before and that her decision to put an end to a tepid unsatisfactory affair had never happened? She brought her mind back to the flat even tones. 'I've been having a chat with her about the house I'm thinking of buying, out in the suburbs, and she agrees it's a great idea, not too far out of the city for both of us to go in to work each day——' Her incredulous expression must have got through to him at last, for his self-satisfied tones broke off. He added after a moment. 'That's after we're married and you've got this country stint out of your system. It'll be a holiday for you, this little break.'

The angry words threatened to tumble from her lips, but catching Paula's amused glance, Lanie fought for control.

'It's temporary domestic work,' she wished she could control the betraying wobble in her voice, 'and we're not engaged to be married any more, remember?'

It was no use, she thought despairingly. Trevor was eyeing her with the indulgent glance of a parent coping with a difficult child. 'We have our little upsets once in a while,' he appealed to Paula, 'don't all engaged couples? But they don't mean a thing. It all comes out right in the end. That's why I'm going back to put a deposit on the house. I'll never get the chance of a bargain like this again, and you have to grab opportunities when they fall into your lap!'

'I'm with you there!' Paula sent him a sparkling glance. She was enjoying her discomfiture, Lanie thought hotly, and doing her best to encourage Trevor.

To change the subject Lanie rushed into speech. 'How on earth did you get here so quickly?'

He was looking as stupidly self-satisfied as ever. 'Took off as soon as I could. When I rang you in town I caught you at an awkward moment with you just leaving the flat, but I knew if I could see you again we'd straighten everything out.'

'No, we can't!' Lanie's low troubled tone didn't appear to penetrate his self-opinionated attitude. Nor did he seem to notice her tightly set lips and flushed cheeks.

She wrenched her mind back to Paula's voice. 'Why not stay here for a day or two?' she was saying with her brilliant smile. 'Jard has endless folk popping in and out—I'm on a visit myself, actually. There's swags of room in the homestead, and out in the waybacks like this, you won't come across any other accommodation. It's the only way——'

To Lanie's dismay, he leaped at the opportunity Paula had handed to him. 'I'd like that.'

'Come along, then.' Paula rose, stretching her arms lazily above her head. 'I'll see you to the guest room, or one of them. Did you bring a bag with you?'

He nodded. 'I was planning on putting up at a motel for the night.'

She laughed.

'Not around here you won't! Jard runs the only motel around in this district. You might as well stay for the night,' she ran on, 'everyone else does. Who knows,' the dark eyes flashed a taunting glance in Lanie's direction, 'you might even enjoy the cooking!'

'Thanks very much. I'll take you up on that.'

Why was he thanking Paula? Lanie wondered resentfully. This wasn't her home, so why was she being so free with her invitations? Unless—— She wrenched the unwelcome explanation aside and brought her mind back to Trevor's ponderous tones. 'I'll get my bag from the car.'

'I'll come with you.' Lanie sprang to her feet. Somehow she had to see Trevor in private and make him see the true position between them. Already he had given Paula the impression that they were a couple engaged to be married and parted only by a temporary rift.

'You don't seem all that glad to see me,' he was saying in an aggrieved tone as they went up the long hall together. 'I thought you'd at least look a bit pleased that I was here.'

'Pleased!' She flung around to face him, all the suppressed frustration of the last few minutes bursting out in a flood of anger. 'Of course I'm not pleased to see you! Chasing after me all this way, giving people here the wrong impression about us, about everything— how did you get my address anyway?'

'No problem.' He was positively smirking. 'I asked your friend Ann at the office. Now all I have to do is to convince you I'm willing to overlook all that nonsense of yours about breaking things off between us. I really mean it.'

'Oh, I know you mean it,' she said in a low tone. Why hadn't she realised long ago that Trevor was interested only in his own concerns? 'It's what *I* think that I'm trying to get through to you!'

'You'll come around all right.' He was as supremely egotistical as ever, she thought frustratedly.

They had reached the dust-coated car and she put a hand on his arm. 'It's all over—*over*. Can't you understand? We had this all out in town——'

'Oh, that——' He brushed aside her words as of no consequence, his colossal self-importance reasserting itself. 'You were a bit uptight that night, had a big day at the office. I knew once you'd had time to think things over you'd feel differently. That's why I came after you. I'll tell you something,' he accorded her an indulgent grin. 'It was a good thing we had that little upset in a way, it made us appreciate each other!'

Lanie drew a deep breath. 'Look, I'm serious about this, I really am——'

'At this moment, maybe, but later when we've thrashed things out we can make a new start. Just wait until the news gets around the grapevine at the office that two of their staff are teaming up with wedding bells, the new house, the lot!'

'You're fooling yourself,' she said on a sigh. It seemed that nothing but the truth would get through to him. 'It's over,' she said gently. 'You've just got to face up to it.'

'If I thought for one moment you meant it——'

'I do!'

'We'll see.' It was incredible, she thought helplessly, that Trevor simply refused to take her seriously.

Later that day, when Trevor had showered and rested in his room, he came into the kitchen where she was starting to prepare the evening meal. Soon he was following her around, cheerfully discussing the house he was thinking of buying, with utter disregard of her stormy silence. As she peeled potatoes and kumeras and put them in the roasting pan in the oven with a leg of hogget, she had difficulty in keeping her mind on her tasks. He was making her so *mad*! 'We'll talk about it later,' she said shortly.

Clara, coming into the room with a Maori flax kit bulging with freshly picked beans and peas from the garden, paused in surprise at sight of the stranger in his dark suit. She glanced enquiringly from Trevor to Lanie's mutinous expression and heightened colour.

'This is Clara,' Lanie told Trevor. 'She's the housekeeper here.'

Clara nodded pleasantly. 'We're used to seeing strangers popping in and out. You're——?'

'Lanie's fiancé,' Trevor supplied. Did he really

imagine, Lanie thought crossly, that saying the words could somehow make them come true, wipe out the past few days?

'No! I'm not——' She broke off, aware of Jard's enigmatic gaze. Lean, rangy, ever so tall, he was standing in the doorway, taking in the little scene.

'Jard,' Lanie said breathlessly, 'this is——'

'Trevor's the name!' How flabby and pale were Trevor's hands, Lanie thought. And how lifeless his handshake in Jard's sinewy grip.

'I saw there was a strange car out in the drive.' Jard was speaking easily, almost friendly to her for once, Lanie realised. 'You two will have a lot of things to talk about.' His gaze swept towards Trevor. 'No need for you to go hurrying back to town—we can put you up for the night,' his mocking glance returned to Lanie's flushed face, 'dinner and all! If you're in luck, Trevor, Lanie'll put on something special, like a celebration dinner.' She threw him an angry look. He was mocking her, darn him. He knew she wasn't a cook, not a proper one. The thoughts ran through her mind. Why did Jard seem so pleased to have Trevor here? Was it because he had overheard Trevor referring to her as his fiancee? Well, she vowed, she would soon disillusion him on that score, once she had got through to Trevor that their association was over, no matter how hard he tried to make himself believe the contrary.

Her preparation of the evening meal wasn't helped by Clara, who was fluttering about, saying at intervals: 'Edna doesn't do it like that.' Until in the end Lanie's taut nerves snapped. 'I don't care how she does it!' she cried crossly. 'This is the way I do it!' Clara's face puckered and immediately Lanie regretted her moment of anger.

'It's okay, love. I know how you must feel with your fiancé coming all this way to see you and you stuck in the kitchen. It's enough to make any girl feel mad!'

Lanie's smile was rueful. If only her relationship with Trevor were as simple as that, how easily her problems would be resolved.

In her haste and confusion she didn't attempt to make a dessert but mixed custard powder in milk and opened a jar of preserved peaches from the stock she discovered on high shelves. Clara eyed her reprovingly. 'Edna always uses fresh fruit when it's in season. She keeps those for emergencies.'

'This is an emergency!'

Clara subsided. 'Of course, love, I understand.'

The meal Lanie served that evening, if not inspiring or adventurous, was at least satisfying, she decided. The meat was cooked to tender succulence, the roasted vegetables crisp and golden, and you couldn't go far wrong with beans and peas freshly picked from the garden. Yet to Lanie the food had no taste and she picked at her plate, longing for the time to pass when she could at last straighten matters out with Trevor. She was only half aware of the conversation echoing around the table—Paula's spirited account of a horse show she had once attended in England where she had successfully competed against internationally known riders, Jard's deep attractive tones as he explained to Trevor the advantages of the use of aerial topdressing on the high hills surrounding the station.

When at last she began to clear away the coffee cups, Clara came hurrying towards her. 'Look, love, your boy-friend has come all this way to see you, so don't you worry about the dishes. I'll see to them.'

'Thanks a lot, Clara. I'll just clear away.'

Trevor followed her into the kitchen. 'That was a pretty good effort of yours.' He was looking as smug, she thought crossly, as if she had prepared the meal especially for him.' I never knew you could rustle up a meal like that. A real celebration spread!'

Her soft lips tightened and she flung around to face him.

'Whatever gave you that idea? I do the cooking around here, I told you, it's my job!'

'Off you go, you two!' Clara smiled conspiratorially towards Trevor. 'No lovers' quarrels in the kitchen! I'll take over here while you take Lanie out for a stroll. She hasn't even seen the place properly yet.'

'Good thinking!' In two strides Trevor had reached her side, laying a hand on her bare arm. 'Come along. You heard what the lady said? Thanks, Clara.'

They moved away together up the hall, passing the closed door of the lounge room where a popular dance recording echoed from the stereo. Were Jard and Paula dancing to the pulsing beat? Lanie wondered.

Trevor's insistent voice brought her back to the present. 'I've come to tell you to give up this crazy idea. You're wasting your time, messing about with housework——'

'It isn't housework, it's cooking——'

'Let them find someone else. It won't matter to them, but I,' all at once his voice thickened, 'I guess I need you. No one else will ever take your place with me, Lanie.'

She ignored his last words. 'No, I promised. I won't let them down.'

'What about me? You don't seem to mind letting me down!'

'I'm not—Oh, what's the use! You just won't understand!'

They crossed the wide drive, moved through a small gate and were taking a narrow path winding up a grassy rise, but neither were aware of their surroundings. A purple haze lay over the bush in the gullies and a single star glittered in the deep soft blue above. Over it all brooded a stillness, broken only by the distant cry of the native owl from nearby trees, 'Morepork, morepork.'

'This is far enough for me.' Trevor paused in the shelter of a grove of *karaka* trees, then dropped down in the shadows. Swiftly he pulled Lanie down beside him on the dried grass. 'You don't know what it means to me, your trying to break things off——' The ragged tones cracked and suddenly he was clasping her to him in a convulsive grip, raining kisses on her hands, her face, her throat. 'You can't mean what you said . . . tell me it's all a mistake . . . we can start afresh . . .' She barely caught the low muttered words as determinedly she strained away from his grasp. Never in all the time she had known him had she seen him at the mercy of his emotions. His breathing was uneven, his voice hoarse with passion. 'Love me, girl!'

At last she managed to break free of his close embrace. 'It's no use——' All at once her anger died away and in its place came a rush of pity for this man who had for so long kept his deepest feelings locked away.

'I'm not asking you for anything you can't give! We can put off the wedding plans, whatever you say.'

Whatever you say! Lanie could scarcely believe her ears. From Trevor, who as a rule considered only himself. Better to give it to him straight and make the position clear once and for all. 'Don't you see,' she said softly, 'it's all over—*over*. You'll meet someone else——'

'Never! It's you, Lanie. Darling——'

Gently she placed a hand over his mouth. 'It's no use going on and on like this.'

Pushing her hand aside, he carried her fingers to his lips. In a more controlled tone he said persuasively, 'But if you thought it over——'

'But I have,' she cried, 'and the more I've thought about it the more certain I am that I'm doing the right thing! I never dreamed you would follow me all the way down here.'

'I had to make you change your mind about me, about us.' A faint tinge of hope coloured his tone. 'If I can't make you see things my way while I'm here, I'll keep on trying when you come back to town.'

'I'll never feel any differently!' She added thoughtfully, 'And I've got a funny feeling that I won't ever work in the city again. Somehow since coming here I've realised I'm a sort of country person really. I know I don't look it, but I am. I like it here. Rangimarie might be the back of beyond, edge of the world and all that, but somehow,' her voice was dreamy, 'it's my kind of place.'

'It hasn't taken you long to make up your mind about that!' An ugly sneer coloured his tone. 'Your sort of place—or do you really mean your sort of man? The boss of the whole show that you've set your sights on? He gave you the job, he brought you to his home. It hasn't been long, but long enough for you to know that you've got a chance of being on to a good thing, if you play your cards right!'

'Stop it!' Lanie was trembling with rage and indignation. 'You can do what you like,' she said in a low tone. 'I'm going back to the house.'

'Not before you kiss me goodbye!'

She tried to spring to her feet, but Trevor pulled at her hand, holding her prisoner. She had never seen him in this mood, furiously angry and apparently beyond reasoning with.

'Let me go, Trevor!' The words came on a hissed breath. At that moment she hated him. A swift turn and she was free of his grasp and hurrying away. But almost at once he had caught up with her, his breathing heavy, his voice loud and rasping. 'What's your hurry? Even if you have ideas of making up to the great white chief, you can spare me a last goodbye!' She tried to dodge past him, but he was too quick for her. Once again he caught her close, then his mouth came down on hers in fierce and hurtful pressure.

Locked in a tight embrace, neither heard the footfalls of rubber thongs on the grass, and only when a man's tall figure appeared on the path did Lanie realise that Jard was striding past them. A brief ''Night' and he had gone on down the slope.

At last Lanie managed to free herself and put a hand to bruised lips. There was a sick feeling welling up in her midriff. What if Jard had overheard Trevor's damning words about her? Now she was hurrying away in the near-darkness, down the pale glimmer of the pathway. She was running, running in at the gate and into the sanctuary of her own rooms. How could Trevor have made those cruel accusations against her? And what ill fate had brought Jard within earshot in

the stillness of the windless night? Useless to tell herself
that he couldn't possible distrust her any more than he
already did. It didn't help her turmoil of mind, nothing
did. For somehow it had become very important to her
that he should think well of her. Not that it mattered,
she assured herself, but deep down she knew that it did,
it mattered terribly.

She didn't know how long she lay in the darkness,
her mouth dry, going over and over the scene on the
darkening slopes. It seemed to her a long time later
when the revving of a car engine cut across the intense
stillness, and moving to the window she parted the
curtains to see headlamps blazing across the driveway.
The next minute Trevor's car shot away at speed,
clattering over the cattlestop and hurtling around the
curves of the driveway. She stood at the window
watching until the car lights vanished in the darkness
and she knew that Trevor had gained the main road. In
his present black mood she feared for his safety, but the
next minute she told herself that he was much too
mindful of his own wellbeing to take any risks that
might bring injury to himself.

Funny, she mused, how it was Jard's strong
masculine face that stayed in her mind and Trevor, who
had caused such an upset to her nerves today, had
somehow ceased to matter. Already he had become a
part of her old life. Only Jard was important to her, and
that of course was only because he was under such
misapprehensions regarding her. Unconsciously she
gave a deep sigh. And that was something she could do
nothing about.

In the morning Lanie put sizzling hogget chops down
on the breakfast table in front of the two men, Heavens,
she thought, she'd have to come up with a change in the
breakfast menu soon, for even sheep farmers might care
for something different. Apparently, however, they had
no complaints, maybe because this time the food was
sufficiently cooked to be palatable. Sandy, seated
opposite her at the table, was positively beaming.
'You're doing fine, lass. Keep on the way you're going

and you'll make some young farmer a real good wife one of these days!' He sent Jard a teasing glance. 'Don't you agree?'

Jard's answer was a cool nod and the way he was looking at her, Lanie thought, was more disapproving than ever. She braced herself for what was coming.

'Your boy-friend seems to have taken off,' he observed calmly. 'Shot through in a bit of a rush, didn't he?'

Lanie's cheeks flamed. What could she say? 'It was all a mistake,' she said breathlessly, 'his following me down here. Don't worry, he won't bother you again.'

'Doesn't bother me any.' He shot her one of searching glances from all-too-perceptive grey eyes. 'How about you?'

She eyed him steadily, 'Me either,' and sent up a swift prayer. Please God, she thought, let him not have heard those lies Trevor was saying about my staying here because of hopes of a romantic attachment with Jard—or Sandy. I'd die, I'd just die of humiliation if he had.

All at once the crisp toast she was biting into had no taste.

'Suits us,' Sandy was saying in a pleasant, self-satisfied tone. Really, she thought, he was just about purring. 'We don't want our new cook whisked away just when we've taken all the trouble to find her!' At Jard she didn't dare look.

When she did steal a glance towards him he was busy scribbling telephone numbers and names in a jotter pad. What was the matter with her, to imagine the conversation would be of any great interest to the big boss? He was simply indifferent to her. A new and even more depressing thought ran through her mind. Could it be that he was disappointed that Trevor hadn't been able to persuade her to leave the station with him? Trevor . . . she writhed inwardly at the thought that he had taken trouble to confide in everyone here, giving them the impression that he and she were still planning their marriage. That this stint in the country was a mere impulse and the really important things in her life were

Trevor, marriage, their new home.

At that moment she became aware that Paula had come into the room, black hair swinging to her shoulders. How was it, Lanie wondered, that the other girl managed to resemble fashion models one saw in the display windows of city boutiques, even when wearing an open-necked shirt and blue jeans?

'Hi, folks!' Paula called gaily, but her smile was all for Jard. She helped herself to coffee, then turned to Lanie. 'Morning! What have you done with Trevor? His car seems to be missing from the driveway.'

As if you didn't know. Wildly Lanie sought in her mind for a suitable explanation. 'He had to go back to town unexpectedly.'

Paula raised pencilled eyebrows. 'I'll say he did! I thought you two were all set for wedding bells and all the rest of it.'

Lanie averted her face. 'Not any more,' she said, and realised the next moment that in her confusion she had put the matter in the worst possible light. Now everyone here would think——

'I'm off home for a while,' Paula was saying, 'until I get problems again, Jard. I couldn't sort them out without your good advice. Now I know that you approve of the mare——'

'I'll give you a hand to load her on the float.' He had risen to his feet, tall, browned, by the summer sun and somehow immensely impressive, Lanie conceded to herself reluctantly. She brought her mind back to Jard's tones. 'If she's anything like the last thoroughbred you brought along, we're in for quite a performance.'

'Nothing we can't handle between us. 'Bye, Sandy, see you at the weekend. 'Bye, everyone.' Her careless gesture of farewell included Lanie and Clara.

Left alone at the table, Clara stared after the man and girl who were passing through the gate and taking the path leading to a big transporter parked near the stables.

Lanie waited for Clara to make mention of Trevor's sudden departure, but evidently the older woman was tactfully avoiding any mention of the matter. 'Thought she was never going,' she muttered darkly. 'Just because her sister was welcome as the day, she seems to think it's all the same with her and Jard——' She broke off, and something stronger than her avoidance of gossip brought the words to Lanie's lips.

'Maybe she's right about that.'

Clara looked thoughtful. 'Don't ask me. He's always nice to her, helps her with everything, horses, stock buying, investments, the lot—but then he'd do the same for anyone who needed help. He's like that. He'll go out of his way to give a hand to anyone who needs it.'

Lanie blinked. It was scarcely her experience of her employer, but she remained silent. 'He seems to like her all right,' Clara was saying, 'but he's known her for all those years, ever since she was a kid coming home for holidays from boarding school. I can see,' she mused aloud, 'that he'd have a soft spot for her because of her sister, but if she thinks she can twist him around her little finger the way she has with the other men friends she's had ... Maybe that's what attracts her to him. She can't ever push him around. With Jard you never can tell. He might like her a lot or he might not, but it's my belief she's crazy about him, and always has been. She's been engaged twice, but each time it was broken off by her. If you ask me, she can't get him out of her heart—My goodness,' she poured herself a second cup of tea, 'I'm getting as soppy as Edna with her brides— you must have noticed all the wedding photographs in her room?'

Lanie laughed. 'There are an awful lot of them, and so many years apart!'

'I know. She's such a practical soul, you have no idea. One of those no-nonsense sort of people, downright and all that. But she has this thing about weddings—must be a romantic at heart! The photographs of the brides and grooms are all relations of hers, some of them she hadn't seen in years, but at the sight of a wedding invitation she would drop everything and go! Every once in a while she has a visit from some of them. I never recognise the women without their wedding finery, or the men either, for that matter. It was the same with this niece in London,' she ran on. 'Edna had only seen the girl once, and that was when she was a baby. Then the family went overseas to live and they didn't correspond. Then out of the blue came this wedding invitation all the way from England. The ceremony was to be held in three weeks' time and I couldn't help thinking that maybe Edna's sister-in-law was hoping for a nice wedding gift from New Zealand without the expense of an extra guest. But they didn't know Edna. She wrote right back accepting the invitation and saying she was coming to stay with her in-laws for a month. I bet that rocked them!

'Anyway, she got a booking on Air New Zealand and managed to get away just before the air strike, or we hope she has. She planned to stay with her sister in Auckland for a few days before the plane was due to leave. Before we realised what was happening, she'd gone, and Jard had to rush up to town to try and get someone to fill in.' Clara's small face broke into a friendly smile. 'I'm glad it was you.' Immediately she spoiled the compliment by adding uncertainly, 'Though I don't know what Edna would think, your being so young and all——'

Lanie wrinkled her nose at her. 'Does it matter?'

'I suppose not.' Clara's voice was dubious, and Lanie got the impression that the absent cook brooked no opposition in her domain.

Standing at the sink bench while Clara dried the breakfast dishes, Lanie couldn't tear her glance away from Jard and Paula. They were chatting together and neither appeared to be at all anxious to part company. Presently, however, they loaded a spirited black mare up a ramp and into the shining transporter, and still Jard lingered. Clearly he was deep in conversation with the girl seated in the driver's seat of the vehicle. Couldn't he bear to part with her? Heavens, she chided herself the next moment, she was becoming as gossipy and foolishly sentimental as Clara! If this were the effect country living had on her ... Country living, she thought wryly, so far as she was concerned, had consisted of being in the kitchen and dining room with brief trips to her own rooms. Soon, she promised herself, when she had become more used to her cooking stint, she would have more time. She would ask Sandy to find her a horse to ride, then she would really begin to enjoy herself. The nice thing about this visit was that she had weeks and weeks ahead of her. It was only Jard's presence that spoiled her enjoyment. She would put him out of her mind and concentrate on just *being here*. It was the oddest thing, she thought a little later as she mixed scone dough in a basin, how much at home she felt here already. Maybe it was because she was a country girl at heart—and she had only just realised it!

As she watched the transporter moving up the winding drive and then turn into the lonely, bush-fringed road a sudden inexplicable happiness surged through her. Because Trevor had at last accepted her decision for them not to meet again? Or could it be, the sneaky thought came unbidden, because Paula had left Rangimarie to return to her own home?

She was working in the kitchen an hour later when Jard entered the room, sending her senses spinning in wild confusion. Had he overheard Trevor's wildly shouted words to her last night on the dark slope, she wondered, or hadn't he? She thrust the thought away, realising that Jard had brought a companion with him, a deeply tanned young man with a shy grin and a boy's lanky frame.

'Lanie,' said Jard, 'this is Brent. He's got himself a job with us as stockman. Lanie looks after the cooking,' he explained, 'with a bit of help, that is.' His quizzical gaze rested on the cookbook lying open on the table. It features all mutton recipes and was entitled *Mary Had a Little Lamb*. The stranger took her hand in his crushing grip.

'Look after Brent, will you,' Jard was saying. 'I expect he wouldn't say no to a cuppa!'

Lanie nodded. 'I'll switch on the jug.' Already she

had learned an unwritten law of the station, that callers were always welcomed to the house with a drink of hot tea or coffee.

'Come down to the stockyards when you're ready,' Jard told the new stockman, 'and I'll fix you up with a job—see you!' He turned away, and Lanie gestured Brent to a seat.

'I won't be a minute,' she told him. Why was it, she wondered, that she felt a sense of constraint only with Jard? There she went again, she *must* drag her thoughts away from him. 'Have you come far?' she asked Brent smilingly.

'Far enough.' Something in the modest tones made her suspect that the answer was an understatement. She sent him a laughing glance. 'Like over the other side of the ranges?'

'That's right. I brought my dog team and my horse with me. Thought it was worth giving it a go, trying for work here,' he was stirring sugar in his steaming cup. 'They tell me that if a man can jack up a job with Jard Sanderson on Rangimarie station he'll learn more in a year than anywhere else in double the time. So I gave in my notice where I was and tried my luck.' *Lucky*, to work for Jard! Lanie kept the disloyal thought to herself.

Because he looked young and somehow lonely, she left the pastry she had been rolling out and dropped down to a seat at the table opposite him. 'How long were you working on the other station?'

Her genuine interest seemed to spark off an eager response. 'Two years as a shepherd.' He smiled at her surprised glance. 'I'm not really a kid, I just look that way. It was okay,' he went on after a moment, 'the boys were a good crowd and we got on fine in the bunkhouse. Then a year ago I was posted out to bush country, miles from civilisation, away from any human contact. At first I liked the sense of remoteness, but lately I got the feeling—well——' her undivided attention seemed to spur him on to confide in her, 'I was getting so I didn't know how to communicate with folk, turning into a loner.' He smiled selfconsciously, an endearing smile, Lanie thought. 'I strum the old guitar a bit and I wrote a song about how I felt alone out there with just the stars at night. Guess it was the loneliness that got me going.'

Lanie leaned both elbows on the table, hands under her chin as she studied his downcast face. 'I'd love to hear it, that song of yours.'

All at once his eyes were alight. 'You don't mean that?'

'I do—honestly!'

'Right now?'

'This minute!'

He sent her a shy grin. 'You've asked for it—look, I'll go and get my guitar, parked it by the back door.' He was hurrying away, a tall gangling youth with a thin frame.

Back in the kitchen he dropped down to a chair. To her surprise he appeared to have lost his selfconsciousness, work-roughened fingers plucking idly at the strings of the guitar. 'Sure you want to hear this?' His anxious gaze pleaded for reassurance.

She nodded smilingly, 'I can't wait!'

The next moment the lilting notes fell on the air and his voice, a surprisingly sweet tenor, took up the melody. At last the notes fell into silence.

'I like it!' Lanie's voice rang with enthusiasm. 'It's good strong country music. I can almost hear the footbeats in the rhythm and the loneliness and the feeling of being at the edge of nowhere—Oh, I don't know how to put it into words. Somehow it touches me——'

'Gee, thanks!'

It was true what she had told Brent, Lanie mused a little while later when he had left the house and she found herself humming the melody as she rolled out pastry for a pie and put it in the oven.

To her relief the mutton pie was a success, and after lunch was over and dishes cleared away she wandered outside past the long line of kennels for the sheepdogs

and down towards the stables. When she reached the
garages she stepped inside the building, looking around
her at a red tractor, a battered truck, a long modern
car. She was about to turn away when masculine voices
reached her through the dividing wall and she guessed
that two young shepherds were also in the garage. The
next minute she realised they were talking about Brent.
'Looked pretty young, for all that riding experience he's
been shouting a line about.'

A second voice: 'You've only got to take one look at
him to see he's just a kid, back from his first stint on a
hill-country station. Well, we'll soon start educating
him——'

'Wait until we give him that unbroken nag. He'll take
our word for it that it's just one of the station
hacks——'

'He'll soon find out——'

'And how! That black devil lets you get up on the
saddle, then *wham*!'

Guffaws of laughter followed.

Lanie shrank back in the shadows. She couldn't
divulge her presence without letting the young
shepherds know that she had overheard their
conversation. All she could do was to stay quietly here
and hope they would soon go away. But if they
imagined they were going to get away with the cruel
joke they were planning to play on that young
stockman—— She would warn Brent about it and he
would make an excuse to avoid the dangerous
encounter.

A masculine voice cut across her thoughts. 'Let's get
cracking or we'll miss all the fun! There's Rob bringing
the horse down from the paddock now. Better get down
there and be ready to pick up the pieces!'

Lanie had to force herself to wait in her hiding place
until the two shepherds moved away. She thought
swiftly, they're going in the direction of the stockyards.
Brent could be thrown and really badly hurt, if he's not
warned in time. Somehow she had to reach him before
it was too late. She began to run and as she came in

sight of the yards she caught sight of Brent's lanky figure. He was perched on the railings by a grassy enclosure, waiting.

The sound of a vehicle behind her made her glance over her shoulder to see Jard at the wheel of his car, a huge woolly sheep in the passenger seat at his side.

With no thought but Brent's imminent danger she planted herself firmly in the pathway and he slowed to a stop, regarding her in some surprise. 'Lanie! What's the hurry?'

'Jard——' she was out of breath, 'you've got to help me! Drive me down to the stockyards—it's ever so important!'

'Okay, I'm on the way there myself. If you don't mind taking a back seat. It's Rutherford——' He threw open the rear door.

Swiftly she clambered into the car. 'Why, is he special?'

'Is he ever? I've specially imported Rutherford. I'm trying out an experiment with Drysdale rams with the idea of producing specially strong carpet wool——'

Lanie scarcely took in his words, her mind too taken up with her own problem to care about the huge woolly animal beside him. Jard started up the car. 'What's the trouble?' His laconic tone only served to intensify her sense of urgency.

'It's that new boy, Brent.' She threw him a harassed glance. 'I've got to warn him! I couldn't help overhearing something the other stockmen were saying. They're going to put him on an unbroken horse, only he won't know about that, just to see if he can ride as well as he says he can!'

'I wouldn't worry about young Brent,' came Jard's drawling voice, 'he can look after himself.'

'But he doesn't *know*,' she cried. 'He won't be prepared! He could be killed in that first moment after he gets up in the saddle!' She was too distraught to choose the words that burst from her lips.

'You're a bit too late to do the lifesaving bit anyway!' With a sinking heart she realised Jard was right. A group of men had gathered at the railings of the enclosure, and even as they drew up at the stockyards, a black horse was led into the enclosure and Brent's lanky form sprang up into the saddle.

Jard and Lanie reached the railings at the same moment as, in a wild flurry of hooves, the unbroken horse leaped from the ground, bucking and rearing in a wild contained fury and determination. But what was happening? Lanie wondered. She stared wide-eyed as the rider, an arm outstretched and a wide-brimmed felt hat in his hand, remained seated. 'Wouldn't you think,' she breathed aloud, 'that he was glued to the saddle!'

'I told you he could look after himself.'

She threw him an accusing glance. 'You *knew*——? All the time——'

'That's right.'

So only Jard, the thoughts ran through her mind, had failed to be deceived by the new stockman's youthful appearance. She brought her attention back to the wildly prancing, bucking horse. At last, lathered in sweat, the mount quietened and Lanie cheered wildly with the rest of the onlookers as Brent rode quietly around the track. Then he dropped lightly to the ground and led the horse back to the entrance. Definitely, Lanie thought with glee, it was Brent's day!

She turned a sparkling face to Jard. 'Wasn't that fantastic! What a triumph for Brent! You know something,' in her excited state of mind she forgot Jard's suspicious attitude towards her, 'I'm so thankful you didn't get here in time to stop the proceedings. I'm glad we saw it all, you and me!'

She found herself enmeshed in his glance, only his eyes weren't cold any more, they were full of light and something else, an expression that she hadn't ever seen there before. It was only for a moment, then a curtain seemed to fall, leaving his eyes contained and expressionless, just—grey.

'Help!' A look of horror crossed her face and her hand flew to her mouth. 'I've just remembered—I've left a pan with fat in it on a hot element!'

'Keep your fingers crossed.' He had taken her arm and was hurrying her back to the car. They took the curving track at speed and when they reached the house Lanie tumbled out of the vehicle and ran inside. In the smoke-filled kitchen, a tongue of flame leaped from the blackened pan, but before she could reach it a masculine hand whipped the flaming utensil away from the heat and switched off the element.

'Thanks.' Lanie let out the word on a breath of relief.

Jard was flinging open the windows, letting in a rush of fresh air. 'Can't have the place going up in flames!' All at once his expression softened. 'Or you.' His gaze flickered over Lanie's flushed young face and tumbled hair. 'You do try, I'll give you that, Lanie.' His tone was oddly gentle.

Faint praise indeed, so why was she feeling this sudden warm glow spreading through her?

His eyes dropped and she barely caught the low muttered words. 'Your hands!' Swiftly she thrust them behind her, all too aware of broken fingernails, discoloured fingers, cuts and scratches, a long burn mark covered in plaster. She might have known it would be useless trying to conceal anything from his probing gaze, for he had grasped her wrists and was examining her small soft hands that a few days earlier had been meticulously cared for, the nails tipped with rosy varnish. 'Pity.'

'I don't know why they're in such a mess, not like office hands.' She laughed ruefully. 'I keep getting burned somehow. I guess I'm in too much of a hurry to get on with things. But I'll get used to it!' The words came breathlessly, for his clasp was doing odd things to her composure. It was an effort to fight her way through the wild sweet confusion of his touch.

'You're doing fine!' The low words, such commonplace words, deepened the glow inside her. He sent her a swift glance. 'You still want to keep on with the job regardless?'

'Oh *yes*!' Her eyes, alight with enthusiasm, rose to meet his deep intent gaze. 'Just try to fire me!'

He dropped her hands at last and went to perch on the side of the table. 'Your boy-friend,' all at once his tone was cold and impersonal, 'he didn't manage to talk you into going back to town with him? Why was that?'

As if it were anything to do with him! Lanie bit back the indignant words that trembled on her lips. She didn't have to answer that one.

'He told me you were all set to tie the knot before you came down here.' The familiar note of suspicion was back in his tones. As if she were someone who wasn't to be trusted, or believed. The cold inquisition continued. 'What made you change your mind? Nothing personal, was it?'

'Like you?' she flung at him, eyes bright with defiance and anger. The next moment she could have kicked herself for the swift impulsive answer. She couldn't help it, though, he was so damned interfering! As if her personal life were any concern of his! All the same, she'd give anything now to recall her words. What if he thought——

His cool rejoinder made her feel even more wretched. 'That's not what I meant.'

Lanie faced him defiantly, two flags of colour burning high on her cheeks. Her voice was husky with emotion. 'What did you mean then?'

Jard's mobile mouth twisted in a sardonic grin. 'If you don't know——'

So, she thought with a plunge of her spirits, they were once more on the old footing, right where they had started. All at once he was back to being the big boss of the station, his glance impassive. 'Things are okay, then?'

She said very low, 'If you mean the job——?'

His cool glance was daunting. 'What else?' He dropped down from the table and she went to the window, watching him stride away. Her cheeks were still burning. It could be due to the heat of the room— well, it could be! She was angry all over again. For him to practically accuse her of staying on here because of some ridiculous suspicions he seemed to entertain

concerning the relationship between Sandy and herself!
It was too absurd, and terribly difficult to refute. If only
she hadn't given Sandy her promise not to betray his
secret. Or could it be, she faced the appalling thought
that had flickered across her mind, that Jard had
overheard Trevor's damning words on the darkening
slopes last evening? If that were true, she caught her
breath, she had unthinkingly played right into his hands
with her defiant 'Like you?' She thrust the suspicion
away as too devastating a possibility even to think
about.

CHAPTER SIX

ON the following afternoon Lanie was trying her hand at preparing an egg custard while Clara, elbows propped on the table, idly watched her. 'Edna doesn't make it that way,' she observed dubiously.

Lanie, sparked to indignation by the all too familiar refrain, spun around. 'I don't care how she does it!'

'Don't you now?' a strong voice echoed from the open doorway. The next moment a big woman with iron-grey hair pulled back in a bun and a no-nonsense expression marched determinedly into the room.

'Edna!' Clara's tone was incredulous. 'What in the world——'

Edna, the station cook, who was thought to be in England! Lanie felt a pang of disappointment out of all proportion to the cause.

'I didn't ring through to Jard first,' Edna was saying. 'I was going to, and then I got the offer of a lift part of the way, so I stayed at a hotel for the night and hired a taxi for the rest of the way. The taxi cost me the earth, but it's a lot cheaper than taking a trip to the other side of the world!'

'But what happened?' Clara asked eagerly.

Edna lowered herself into a chair and fanned her hot face with her hand. 'Well, first of all I was held up by the air strike, but that wasn't too bad because I stayed with my cousin in Auckland. Then when I got word the plane was scheduled to leave I rang through to my relations in London to tell them when to meet me at Heathrow. Seems,' she said grimly, 'they were just going to try and contact me to ask me not to come.'

Clara was hanging on Edna's words. 'Why ever not? Don't tell me——'

'You've guessed it! Seems the wedding's off. My niece has run off with another man. Silly girl, why couldn't she have made up her mind in the first place instead of putting everyone to all this trouble!'

'But surely,' Clara said, 'you could have stayed with your relatives just the same?'

Edna's tone was uncompromising. 'Whatever for? It was the wedding that I was making the trip for, not just to sit around the house twiddling my thumbs. My sister was always one to take on if anything went wrong with her plans. She wouldn't want me hanging around the place just now.' With grudging admiration she ran on, 'Looks as though you've been filling in pretty well here, all on your own too. I didn't think Jard would have any luck in finding anyone who'd be willing to come all the way down here just for a temporary job. He didn't get anyone to suit, evidently——'

'Well,' Lanie's eyes were twinkling, 'there's me!'

'You?' Edna stared at her in disbelief. Clearly, Lanie mused, her youthful appearance had once again proved deceiving. 'But I thought you were some friend of Jard's . . . a visitor here.'

A swift pain shot through her. A friend of Jard's. If only she were! She forced her voice to a matter-of-fact note. 'I got the job in town, and Jard and Sandy brought me down here just after you left.'

She realised, however, that Edna had ceased to listen, her gaze moving past Lanie to settle on the gleaming new electric range. 'What on earth,' Edna demanded, 'is that monstrosity doing in my kitchen?'

Lanie's mouth twitched. 'It's mine—I brought it with me. But it's not connected up yet.' She saw Edna's stern expression relax. 'Jard's arranged for the electrician to come here next week—but I guess,' in spite of herself a forlorn note crept into her voice, 'it won't matter now.'

Edna sniffed. 'It certainly won't!' Something in Lanie's expression, the droop of the soft lips, must have got through to the older woman, for she said in a milder tone, 'It looks as if——'

'I know, I'll have to go.' Lanie couldn't understand why the thought brought with it such a flood of dismay.

'One thing,' Edna was saying in her forthright tones,

'if you want a country job you'll be snapped up in no time! And you don't need to stick to cooking either. There's household help, correspondence supervisor for the kids, farm work. Put an ad in the local rag and you'll find you'll be able to pick and choose what you want.'

'I guess so.' Even in her brief stay here Lanie had learned of the scarcity of home helpers in the remote district. So why did she feel this sense of desolation, as though she were losing something unbelievably precious? The answer came in a flash. Now she would have to say goodbye for ever to any hopes she might have had of making Jard realise that his suspicions of her were utterly unfounded. Jard . . . She was only half away of Edna's tones as she went on to tell her friend about her stay in the city and how relieved she was to return to her familiar environment. There was really nothing to compare with life at Rangimarie, Edna declared. Presently she rose to her feet. 'Well, I'd better go and change——'

Lanie said quickly, 'I've been using your rooms. Jard thought you wouldn't be needing them for a while.'

Edna gave a harsh cackle of laughter. 'First time I've ever known Jard to be wrong! Well, not to worry. You're not very big and you can have the spare room until you leave here and go somewhere else. Don't bother shifting your things right now.'

Somewhere else. To Lanie the words pinpointed with sickening emphasis that this was no longer her home. She must have been crazy to feel as though it were, even if only temporarily. She wrenched her mind back to the present, realising Edna was standing by the window. 'Is Jard around? I'd better go and tell him I'm back.'

Lanie shook her head. 'He's way up on a hill at the burn-off.'

'Oh well, it'll keep.'

'Thank heaven this is the last time I'll have to hump this lot around!' Edna picked up her suitcase and Lanie watched her cross the strip of grass outside, a heavily-built woman wearing a floral silk dress and sensible flat-heeled shoes.

A few moments later Clara followed her. Left alone in the kitchen, Lanie forgot about her custard preparations. She was twisting a strand of hair round and round her finger worriedly in an unconscious gesture. It was over, her lovely new life, almost before it had started, and even Sandy, whose warm championship had never failed her, would be unable to have her kept on now. What an opportunity this would be for the big boss himself! It was what he had wanted all along, and now fate in the form of Edna's fickle niece had played into his hands. As she pictured Jard's triumphal reaction to the news, determination rose in her. She'd beat him to it. She refused to tamely wait around until he returned to the house and gave her her marching orders. Just for once, she told herself, she would call the tune.

Moving to the window, she glanced towards a cloud of smoke that was rising against the translucent blue of the sky. The fire looked a long way away. She had a dim recollection of Sandy telling her that a lot of the hill country of the station was in scrub, high *manuka* trees twenty feet high, and that Jard tackled a block of scrub every year. Her soft lips firmed. Now she was about to tackle him! She pushed the hair back from her hot forehead. She had only to borrow a horse to ride, and that shouldn't be too difficult. All that mattered to her now was that she must let him know she was leaving Rangimarie before he heard the news from someone else. What matter that the smoke clouds she could see billowing from high slopes appeared to be some distance away? She would get there, she *had* to! Soon she was out of the house and hurrying down the curving driveway towards the stables where she could see two of the station hacks already saddled and tethered to a fence. Luck was with her, she thought a short time later as Brent emerged from the stables and strolled towards the horses.

'Brent! Wait——' When at last she reached him she was almost too breathless to speak coherently. 'I'd like one of the horses to ride. Do you think——'

He caught on immediately, his young face curious,
but he made no comment beyond: 'Sure, take Blaze, he
seems quiet enough. You won't have any cause to bale
off him!'

Lanie hesitated, eyeing the massive bay horse. 'He's
not too sluggish?'

He grinned. 'Lord no! He's got a terrific canter.
You'd be surprised! I was just going to take him back
to the paddock, so he's all yours.' He gave her a leg up
into the saddle and handed her the reins. 'Where are
you bound for anyway?'

As she urged the big horse to a trot, she threw back
over her shoulder. 'Just to the burn-off.'

'Hey—wait——' But the wind, blowing endlessly
over the sea, tossed the words away and already she
was moving out of hearing as the big bay horse took a
steep grassy slope threaded with the narrow tracks of a
myriad sheep.

Even in her urgency Lanie was aware of a sense of
exhilaration as her mount scrambled up steep slopes
then plunged down into bush filled gullies, then up and
over another slope where sheep scattered madly at their
approach. When she reached the cleared green strip of
the airfield she let Blaze have his head, leaning forward
in the saddle as the big horse broke into a canter and
then a gallop. The wind tossed the ribbon from her
hair, sending a cloud of reddish-gold streaming behind
her ears as they swept on. All too soon she reached the
shed used for storing topdressing supplies, and once
over the next rise she knew she wasn't far from her
destination. Even from a distance the smell of charred
timber was in her nostrils and an immense pall of
smoke rose ahead.

Presently she neared the burn-off, discerning through
the smoke the great *manuka* trees that had been cut
with a chain saw. Flames were leaping through them
and the crackle was deafening. As she approached,
urging her reluctant mount forward with some
difficulty, she could feel the hot breath of the wind on

her face. On a hilltop overlooking the blazing scrub she drew rein. Not until this moment had she realised how difficult it might be to find Jard amidst the clouds of smoke. Evidently, she thought, the men had relied on the cordon of standing bush to quell the fierce flames, so maybe if she advanced that far she would catch sight of Jard. The next moment she realised that her mount, regardless of his rider's wishes, had no intention of moving any nearer to the leaping flames. The terror-stricken horse was rearing wildly and as she tried to control him a flame, licking through bushes, shot high in the air. Then everything seemed to happene at once as Blaze, half-crazed with terror, reared wildly, and she felt herself flying through smoke-filled air. There was a split-second impression of being tossed down a rocky slope, of clutching desperately at bushes on the way, then blackness, nothingness.

When she returned to consciousness she found herself lying at the foot of a steep cliff. What was she doing here, and why was it so very hot? She raised herself to a sitting position and became aware of long grazes down her arms, of blood trickling from a cut on her ankle, and her head seemed to be beating with tiny hammer strokes. Gingerly she got to her feet, relieved to find she was all right—a trifle wobbly maybe, but there were no bones broken. If only her head would stop throbbing and she didn't have this dizziness. She couldn't even remember how she came to be here, but it would come to her in a minute.

She glanced up at the cliff above. It was almost sheer, with outcrops of rock. No hope of escape that way. A wave of nausea passed over her and she put her head down between her knees. At that moment, above the crackle of the flames on the nearby hillside, she caught the echo of her name. Brent! No one else knew of her intention to come to the burn-off. She raised her head, peering through the smoke at the man's figure she could dimly discern approaching her. Then Jard came hurrying to her side.

'Lanie! Are you all right?' Had she not known the

thought to be absurd, she thought groggily, almost she could have imagined a note of genuine alarm in his tones. He was pulling her to her feet, his strong arms supporting her.

'I wanted to find you,' she said stupidly, 'but I couldn't see you anywhere.'

He wasn't even listening. 'You must have been out of your skull,' he told her angrily, 'to bring Blaze close in to the burn-off! Didn't any of the boys warn you about that? If not I'll have a piece of whoever it was when we get back——' he broke off, his glance moving over her grazed arms and a bruise on her temple. 'You're feeling okay?'

Even in her dazed state of mind she was aware that he was eyeing her with concern—*real* concern, as if she really mattered to him. 'I'll be all right in a minute,' she said thickly, and swayed on her feet as the smoke-screened scene spun dizzily around her.

For answer he gathered her up in his arms and carrying her as effortlessly as if she were a child, strode towards a patch of native bush. 'I've left the Land Rover over there, not far away.'

A blissful feeling of content stole over her as she nestled against his brown, sinewy shoulder. There was a sense of security in being held firmly in his strong arms . . . security and something else, something she couldn't define. Did he *mean* to hold her close, so very close to him? His cotton shirt, open to the waist, was singed with embers of blackened trees and smelled strongly of smoke, yet oddly she didn't mind a bit. Blame that fall down the slopes!

'We'll soon be out into the clearing.' But she knew it wasn't the heat and danger and drifting smoke that was causing her to lie limp and relaxed in Jard's arms but a sheer drugged sensation of deep content. If only, she mused dreamily, he would treat her this way more often, so concerned and protective and unexpectedly tender. Who would have believed that he could set her down so gently in the Land Rover, as if she were made of glass?

She giggled weakly. 'I'm not all that bad.'

'Not all that good either!' He climbed into the driver's seat, threw a steadying arm around her shoulder and set the vehicle in motion. How very different was this ride, the thoughts slid into her mind, from that earlier trip in the Land Rover with him when with reckless abandon he had deliberately sent the vehicle hurtling down sheer slopes. Now he was taking care not to jolt her any more than could be helped. Almost it was worth the accident, she mused, to see the concern in his face.

His voice broke across her musing. 'Does that bruise on your forehead worry you?'

She put a hand to the swelling below her hairline. 'Not really.' *Nothing really worries me right at this moment, Jard, not when I'm here with you.*

'We'll be home soon,' his tone was strangely tender, 'then you can take it easy for the rest of the day.'

Home! The word rang a bell in her heart. She didn't have a home here, not any more. And wasn't that the whole purpose of her ride to the burn-off today to let Jard know what had happened? All at once she was finding it very difficult to find the words, but they had passed the airstrip and were moving into a bush-filled gully in sight of the homestead and she knew she was running out of time. 'I have to go away,' she brought out baldly, and raised herself to glance across at him. 'That's what I was coming to tell you when I got tossed off Blaze.'

'What's got into you, Lanie?' The rough sweetness of his tones was turning her bones to water. A sudden urgency tinged his voice. 'You don't want to go running away, do you?'

'No, no, of course not!' The betraying words were past her lips before she could stop to think.

He drew her close to him and once again the heavenly sense of wellbeing flooded her senses.

'You can forget it! I'll tell you something, Lanie. You're certainly not leaving!'

She eyed him in blank astonishment. 'Why not?'

'I won't let you go, that's why!' His smile was so warm it took her breath away. 'I do the hiring and the firing, remember? Right now you're hired!'

If only it weren't so hard to get through to him. She jerked her mind back to the vibrant masculine tones.

'Anyway, what gave you that crazy idea?' All at once his expression hardened. 'You haven't fallen out with Sandy?'

'No, I haven't!' She flung the words at him. So he still suspected her of some relationship with his father. Oh, she might have known his unfamiliar solicitude was no more than pity because she'd taken a fall. How could she have been taken in by a few words of sympathy? 'If you want to know the reason why I'm leaving,' she tried for dignity, 'it's because Edna came back today. She didn't go to England after all. She walked into the house a while ago, rarin' to get back into her kitchen.'

'You don't say!' Jard gave a shout of laughter. 'Don't tell me—let me guess! The bride had a change of heart at the last minute and took off with another guy?'

Lanie said in surprise, 'How did you know?'

'It sticks out a mile! Nothing but a non-wedding would have stopped Edna's long-overdue trip to England.' He tossed her a sideways grin. 'Don't tell me you haven't noticed the wedding parade plastered over her bedroom walls?'

She had to laugh. 'Have I ever?' Her face sobered. 'So I guess I just—have to go.'

'Who says so?' His tone hardened. 'I take it you've had a word with Sandy?'

She said in surprise, 'Sandy? No, he doesn't know. I wanted to tell you first of all.' It had to be said. 'To give in my notice.'

'You don't sound too happy about it,' Jard observed.

Wildly she sought for an answer. 'I guess I wouldn't feel happy about anything right at this moment.' All at once she was feeling deflated. Where was her moment of triumph? He simply seemed to take for granted her resignation from the job, a nothing thing. To the big boss she was one of his employees, one he had never taken to anyway. Lost in her bleak thoughts, she was scarcely aware of his flat tones. 'We'll talk it over later when you're feeling better.'

He was letting her down lightly, of course. No doubt, she thought angrily, he was feeling relieved at the prospect of having his familiar cook back once more, looking forward to a change of menu. No more half-cooked mutton chops followed by a steady diet of peaches for dessert. All at once the frustrations and disappointments of the day came to a head. To think she had been through so much today to see him, to tell him her news, and it had fallen flat. He didn't even care!

As they went on in silence, taking a Land Rover track over the green sheep-studded slopes, she stole a glance towards him. He was looking straight ahead, his eyes as cold and grey as the tossing sea beneath a sky where gunmetal clouds massed together. 'I'll get another country job,' she said to him, adding with a wry smile, 'now that I've had some experience. That is, if you'll give me a reference? I know I've only been here a week, but——'

'Like I said,' he cut in, and now there was no tenderness in his cool tones, 'we'll talk about it later, when you get rid of that swelling on your head. Leave everything to Edna to cope with tonight. You're to take it easy, right?'

'But I'm not ill or anything——' She made to jerk herself from his grasp, but he pinned her to him even closer.

'That's an order! Hey, look who's heading this way!'

Brent was riding over the brow of the hill. As he came nearer his expression of anxiety faded as he recognised the girl in the Land Rover. Jard pulled the vehicle to a stop as the rider drew rein beside them.

'Lanie!' Brent's voice rang with relief. 'If I'm not glad to see you! Gee, I'm sorry I let you go off on Blaze. If I'd known what I do now about that horse——'

'It wasn't your fault!' Lanie spoke to him from the window. 'The flames suddenly shot up and he took off.

Luckily it was just me and not both of us who went rolling down the cliff. And awfully lucky,' she added warmly, 'that Jard saw me bale out and came to the rescue.'

'Lanie can ride like the wind,' Jard told him. 'Nothing wrong with her riding! She couldn't know that the old devil is paranoid when it comes to fire. Thing is,' he explained to Lanie, 'he had one hell of a fright once and he's never got it out of his system.'

She smiled. 'I'll remember that next time.' Her heart plummeted. Only there wouldn't be a next time. Why must she keep forgetting?

Back in the rooms she now shared with Edna, Lanie was thankful to find the place deserted. Her suitcase, she found, had been moved into the spare bedroom and her dresses and cotton tops were hanging neatly on hangers in the big old-fashioned wardrobe. On the way to the bureau in search of fresh panties and bra she paused, arrested by her reflection in the mirror. Could that really be herself, that scruffy-looking girl whose face was streaked with earth and dried blood, hair entangled with blackened twigs borne by the wind from the blazing hillside. Swiftly she gathered up undergarments and a cotton wrap. She found the first aid kit in Edna's room, then she headed for the bathroom. Soon she was pouring drops of disinfectant into steaming hot water and washing her hair beneath the shower, revelling in the touch of clean soft rainwater.

As she got ready to go to dinner with the others she told herself that tonight she would have need of all the confidence she could summon if she were to give in her notice to Jard before he got in before her and gave her her marching orders. She must look her best, she reflected, running a comb through long red-gold strands that curled damply around her face as if they had a life of their own. The babyish dimples that flickered at the corners of her lips were a definite disadvantage, but those she could do nothing about. Small flames of excitement lighted her eyes, bright with defiance and something else, something she couldn't put a name to.

Tonight she would no longer be the temporary cook—no, sir! She was free. Free to do as she pleased and to look glamorous—well, as glamorous as she could when adorned with odd strips of bandage. Skilfully applied make-up concealed grazes and scratches on her face, then she needed only a touch of mascara to her lashes, a smear of soft pink lipstick on her mouth.

She pulled over her head a filmy blue-grey muslin blouse and tied around her slim waist an ankle-length batik skirt patterned in soft tonings of blues and lilacs. Then she fastened around her throat a necklace of fine silver chains and wriggled her feet into woven string sandals.

Odd to realise that tonight she would have no need to make an appearance at the dining table until the last moment. She would be there just as if she were any ordinary guest at the house, or a friend of Jard's, like Paula, instead of being part of the station work-force.

When she went into the shadowy dining room she was glad she had taken trouble to make herself look attractive, for she was greeted by a startled silence (a tribute to her unfamiliar appearance?). Brent, regarding her with an admiring glance, gave a low appreciative whistle. Immediately Lanie found herself to be the centre of attention. Edna, her face anxious, said, 'I couldn't find the first aid box anywhere!'

'It's all right,' Lanie told her, smiling, 'I helped myself to it.'

'How are you feeling, love, after that accident you had today?' Clara's voice was warmly sympathetic. 'We've been so *worried* about you. When your horse came back without you and no one knew where you'd gone and we couldn't find any of the men. Then Brent came back and he went to look for you. You're not hurt too badly?' Before Lanie could make an answer she added with a glance of appreciation. 'You look all right, anyway. Doesn't she, Jard?' She appealed to the man who was mixing drinks at the cocktail cabinet. Lanie sent Jard a quick glance, but he was standing in the shadows and she couldn't discern his expression.

'Sure! All the same, this should hurry up the healing.' He was crossing the room and handing her a glass.

She eyed him suspiciously. 'What is it?'

'Never mind—down it! You'll feel better for it.'

She wrinkled her nose at him. 'I feel fine——'

'All the same——'

'Oh, all right, then.' She drank the fiery liquid, pulled a face and put down the glass.

At that moment Sandy came into the room, his gaze bent on Lanie. She caught the twinkle in his eyes. 'What's this I've been hearing about you taking a toss and scaring the wits out of everyone around the place, and you a crack rider——'

'I know, I know.' Her bright smile flashed out. 'It was the fire that sent Blaze into a panic. Thank heaven he didn't go plunging down the cliff with me!' A belated sense of gratitude made her add, 'And wasn't I lucky that Jard saw the whole thing even through all that smoke and came to rescue me in the Land Rover!' She raised her glance to meet Jard's deep intent look. Why was he always watching whenever she and Sandy were chatting together?

'So long as you're okay.' She brought her mind back to Sandy's sympathetic tones. He went to pour himself a drink, then returned to her side. 'You wanted to see the burn-off, was that it? Can't say I blame you for that. It's quite a sight, exciting or scary, depending on which way you look at it. When the *manuka*'s tinder-dry like now, it burns like all hell let loose! If it weren't for the cordon of standing bush it would be right out of control.'

'I can imagine.' Lanie dropped her voice to a taut whisper. 'There's something I've got to talk to you about. I can't stay here, not now that Edna's come back. Don't you see——'

'Not to worry, lass.' His comforting tones cut across her distressed whisper. 'Now don't you go tearing off just because things didn't work out the way we thought. Come on now, tell me, you don't want to rush away from here, do you?'

'Not really.' The words seemed to come without her volition. 'But Jard——'

'Never you mind about him! We'll work something out—looks like it's time to start on that soup course that Edna's serving up.'

As she went with him to the table Lanie reflected that he meant well. He was trying to let her down lightly, of course, postponing the moment when he would be forced to come right out with it and bid her goodbye. In the talk and laughter echoing around her, her silence went unnoticed. She was thinking that everyone here would be taking it for granted that she would be leaving very soon now that Edna had returned to be once more in charge of her kitchen.

It was a meal cooked to perfection, yet Lanie found the food to have little taste and she had to force herself to eat. She had only been here a week, she scolded herself, so it was absurd that she should feel this lost sensation about leaving. She made an attempt to boost her sinking spirits. There were other farms and sheep stations who would be delighted to have her work for them in a domestic capacity. What was the matter with her, that Rangimarie held her so? It wasn't even as if the boss wanted her around the station. He'd made no secret of his opinion of her right from the start, and, he'd had no reason since to change his attitude towards her.

The meal seemed to Lanie to last for ever, but at last Jard left the table to go and work in his office, as had been his custom on most nights since she had been here. Brent, excusing himself, went to his own quarters. Edna was carrying out the coffee cups and Clara went to help her.

'Not you, Lanie.' Sandy raised a protesting hand as she made to join the other women in clearing away the dishes. 'You've got yourself a holiday tonight.'

'Thanks, Sandy.' She went to join him in the lounge room, but although she chatted brightly with him, her thoughts were busy. Maybe Jard will come out of the office before long and I'll be able to have things out with him. I'll have to make some arrangements about transport from here, putting an ad in the local newspaper—all that stuff. I don't want to face up to it, but I've got to.

But the time wore on and Jard was still closeted in his office. Edna described to Clara and Lanie her recent stay in the city and Sandy appeared to be intent on the television programmes. Probably, Lanie mused, he was trying to avoid any discussion with her in the matter of her leaving Rangimarie. This time though he could do nothing to help her, not when Jard now had his perfect opportunity to send her packing.

It was late in the evening when the others bade Laine goodnight and drifted away. Left alone, she decided it was useless to wait any longer in the hope that Jard would return to the lounge room. She moved down the long hall and as she neared his office the door was flung open and Jard, tall and impressive, stood in the opening. 'Come in here for a minute, will you, Lanie?'

She drew a deep breath. 'This is it. I won't let him tell me to go!' Resolutely she gathered her defences together and preceded him into a room where the walls were covered with aerial photographs of the station, pictures of horse trials and prize-winning sheep, and clips of files and tallies.

'Take a seat!' He pushed forward a stool and she perched herself on the high seat while he dropped down opposite her on a leather-covered swivel chair.

He faced her across the wide desk, eyeing her with his penetrating look that, as always, did things to her composure and sent her thoughts flying in all directions. *It wasn't fair.* Lanie tried to pull herself together. Could it be the overhead light bulb that lent his face those shadows, making his lean face look stern and angular? 'I know what you're going to say,' she told him breathlessly, 'but it's all right. You don't need to worry. I'll be leaving right away, *I'll have to.*' Now where had those betraying words come from? If only he hadn't noticed the slip. 'Now that Edna's back here again,' she ran on quickly, 'you won't be needing me any more.'

'You reckon!' His smile, that heart-knocking smile that melted all her defences, sent her resolutions from her mind. 'Thing is,' he was eyeing her speculatively, 'how do you feel about taking on something else around the place?'

Taken by surprise, she raised clear green eyes to his gaze, then dropped her glance, unable to sustain his look. She said very low, 'What—sort of something else?'

He waved a lean, darkly tanned hand. 'All sorts. If you'd put me in the picture before about being able to ride——'

She said unthinkingly, 'I thought Sandy would have told you.'

His face tightened and a betraying anger showed in his eyes. He was looking straight at her, his eyes narrowed. 'There are quite a few things he didn't let on to me about.'

Lanie felt the anger rising in her like a dark cloud. She leaned forward, the colour staining her cheeks. 'Are you trying to say——' She broke off in confusion. It was useless. For how could she explain the truth of the matter without letting Sandy down, and after all, he had got her this job in the first place. If only she didn't have this feeling that keeping his secret meant so much to him.

'Let's keep to the point, shall we?' Ice dripped in Jard's tone. This is the moment, she thought, when he's going to tell me to go. There wasn't much comfort in knowing that it had been her own suggestion. She jerked her mind back to the cool, cutting tone.

'Like I said, I can put you on to something else if you're interested.' She was too intent to notice the irony in his voice. 'My dad seems to think you might be.'

Immediately she broke all her resolutions of being offhand, of telling him just where he could take his job. Instead she heard herself saying eagerly, 'Oh, I am, I am! What would I have to do?'

'Whatever happens to be going, actually. What

would you say to giving a hand with shifting stock, checking the dams and the waterholes, riding work mostly.'

'Riding!' She could scarcely believe her luck. Dimples flickered at the corners of her soft mouth. 'Why, that would be super!'

'Award rates, of course,' came the controlled tones, 'plus your keep. You can share the outside quarters with Edna, if that's okay with you?'

'Oh *yes*!' Suddenly she was feeling wildly elated. He had conceded her riding ability, so maybe he really needed her to help him round up cattle on the sandhills, and wouldn't that be fabulous! Bless you, Edna, for cancelling your trip to the wedding over in England! Eyes bright with anticipation, she said eagerly, 'When do I start? Tomorrow?'

'That's right.' He stopped her with his hard tone. 'Daybreak, actually. I'll need you around to give me a hand in the woolshed tomorrow.'

'Me?' She was so surprised the word came out as a squeak.

'Why not?' She surprised a gleam of amusement in his eyes, then it died away as swiftly as it had come and a cool satirical note tinged his tones. 'I have to have someone in the shed with me to sweep up and sort the fleeces.'

'Oh!' She felt a strong desire to kick something. There he went again, cutting her down to size, or trying to. How could he be so lean and tough and heartbreakingly good-looking, yet so deliberately hateful, *and only towards her*! She said slowly, 'You mean you want me in the shed as rouseabout?'

'That's it. I've got a job on tomorrow for a neighbour, an elderly guy on his own who isn't the best since he copped a tractor accident last year. He's got a few sheep that I shear for him in the season. It'll only take a day and I'll need someone to give me a hand to push sheep into the pens——'

'P-push them?'

'You could handle it,' he bent on her his mesmeric

gaze that played havoc with her emotions, 'anyone could.' Unfeeling brute! Lanie jerked her mind back to the cool tones. 'Sandy seems quite confident you can cope.'

Sandy! Oh, she might have known it was only because of his father that he was keeping her on his payroll. The thought sparked her to say defiantly, 'You don't sound very enthusiastic about the idea?'

He shrugged broad shoulders. 'Like I said, anyone could do it—another thing I need to know——' he shot her a swift enquiring glance from penetrating grey eyes, 'do you happen to hold a current driver's licence?'

'Yes, I do.' Now she felt herself on familiar ground. 'I've never owned a car, but I used to take the van sometimes at work when the office manager wanted samples delivered around the city.'

'Tremendous!' He didn't appear, she thought, to be all that excited about her driving ability.

Hope rose in her anew. 'Where would you want me to go? I'd love to drive along the beach——'

'All I want you to do,' his tone was definitely deflating, 'is to take a run up to the house and bring down the smoko.'

'I get it.' She managed to recover herself. 'Well, I guess if I'm going to be rouseabout——'

Jard's voice was deadpan. 'Over to you.'

If he was throwing challenges about, she thought hotly, she would accept them! She schooled her voice to a nonchalant tone. 'Daybreak, you said?'

'Right. That's settled, then.' He rose from his chair and strode forward to open the door for her.

''Night, Lanie.'

She hesitated, sending him a quick upward glance. If only you'd smile when you say it, Jard, the way you smile for other folk, for Paula. Just once. But taking in the hard unyielding lines of his face she knew it was wishful thinking. She turned away. 'Goodnight.'

CHAPTER SEVEN

LANIE was so fearful of sleeping in in the morning that she awoke long before the time set on her small travelling alarm clock. Swiftly she dressed, pulling on shabby jeans, a loose shirt of white cotton, slipping her feet into rubber thongs. Her bright hair she coiled in a knot on top of her head to give some protection from the dust and wool of the shearing shed.

Through the window she could see a tumble of pink clouds that heralded the sunrise, hear the boom of the surf on the sands that mingled with the lowing of cattle and the crying of seabirds. For no reason at all she felt a surge of happiness. Today, on this freshest of mornings, where the bush in the gullies was veiled in mist and the hills sharply outlined against the translucent tender blue of the sky, just being here was sufficient to send her spirits soaring. It's a new world to me, the thought sang through her mind, and I love it! Even the prospect of working under the directions of the boss in the hot shed down on the beach couldn't dim her newly-found happiness. She picked up her denim cap and pulled it over her hair. Tendrils of red-gold escaped and she tucked them determinedly out of sight.

As she reached the back door of the homestead she ran into Jard, and for a moment their glances held. In that instant some irresistible force quivered between them, something that made Lanie's pulses leap and sent vibrations quivering along her heartstrings. To break the moment of awareness she jerked her peaked cap over one eye, planted her feet together and raised a hand to her forehead in a mocking salute. 'Reporting for duty—sir!'

A reluctant smile played around his lips and almost she could read his thoughts. She won't be feeling so cheeky after a gruelling day's work in the hot woolshed.

'I was just on my way over to give you a call. Edna's got breakfast on the table.' This time he sent her a real grin. 'How does that strike you?'

'Just fine.' She smiled back at him. It must be the effect of the breathless morning air, she told herself, that was giving her this sense of heightened perception as if everything in the world were suddenly fresh and new, even Jard's feeling for her.

Edna, who evidently believed in a rouseabout being fed in the same manner as the rest of a shearing gang, had dished up a massive meal of chops, sausages and egg. Lanie did her best with the egg and tried to avoid Edna's disapproving glance.

Presently she went with Jard to the car waiting in the driveway, eyeing his well-shaped hands as he worked the controls. She was trying to memorise the gear movements which fortunately appeared to be the same as the van she had driven. With Jard, she reminded herself, you had to be one step ahead. She had a suspicion that his present pleasant mood wasn't going to last for ever. It didn't. The next moment his tone was definitely that of a boss giving orders to one of his staff. 'I'd better give you the run-down on what you have to do——'

'I know,' she cut in, and rattled off quickly: 'Push sheep into the pens for you to shear, sweep up the wool and sort it out on the table, go up to the house in the car and bring back smoko——'

'You've got it.' They were taking a curving track cut through sandhills and leading to the grassy flats by the sea. As they swept down the rise Lanie glimpsed the bleached logs piled up on black sandhills of glittering ironsand, the tossing surf and the fiery ball of the sun flaming over the horizon.

Presently they were approaching the drafting pens adjoining the old timbered woolshed. Jard braked to a stop and soon they were mounting the *kauri* steps leading up to the shed. At that moment however a truck came roaring down the slope and Lanie went with Jard down to the yards where the driver was unloading sheep from his truck.

'Right.' He was a young man with twinkling dark eyes and a friendly grin. 'They're all yours, Jard——' He couldn't seem to take his gaze from Lanie's face.

Briefly Jard made the introduction. 'Mervyn, this is Lanie.' He added carelessly, 'Lanie's my rouseabout.'

The stranger looked surprised. 'You could have fooled me!' His appreciative glance was taking in Lanie's clear skin and trim figure, the expression of excitement that lit her small face. 'I would never have thought——'

'Let's get cracking, shall we?' Jard cut in impatiently. He was giving some 'hurry-up' to the ewes he was guiding into a pen.

'See you.' With a lingering glance in Lanie's direction and a lift of his hand, the driver swung the truck around and took the sandy track along the beach.

Lanie had already forgotten him. She was moving with Jard up the steps of the shed once again. She glanced up into his closed face and once again the inexplicable surge of wild sweet happiness coursed through her. It must be something about the freshness of this magical morning, alive with birdsong from the trees around them. 'He didn't look geriatric to me!' she teased. She mocked in her sweet husky tones, '"Not up to doing much around the place" was the impression I got, from what you told me about your neighbour.'

Jard glanced down at the lively little face beneath the jauntily set cap and a flash of humour chased across his features. 'True, true.' In the end it was Lanie who dropped her lashes and looked away. At last, she thought triumphantly, she had got through to him, and couldn't resist the temptation of adding, 'The way he was tossing those sheep about, he looked healthy enough to me!'

'Oh, he is.' Jard's voice was deadpan. 'Only thing is, he's a lawyer who works in Wellington and drops in now and again to spend holidays with his uncle. Shearing sheep isn't his thing.'

'I see.' Privately she was of the opinion that at least Mervyn was pleasant and outgoing. His admiring glance for her had beamed an unmistakable message: 'I'd like to get to know you better.' He had a smile for her too, not like Jard, she mused vindictively, who was nice to her only once in a while and then you could see it was only because he had forgotten to put up his guard. Unconsciously she sighed. If only Sandy hadn't suffered that heart attack!

Jard flung open the heavy doors of the shearing shed and they moved together into the shadowy interior of the building. Her gaze moved over the five stands with their electrical equipment, the great presses and piles of wool bales. 'Right! Let's get on with it!' Jard had paused to pull his T-shirt over his head, emerging with rumpled dark-blond hair, and looking, she thought, more approachable, younger, less Jard-like. Seeing him stripped to the waist, the rippling muscles of his chest and sinewy body tanned as deeply as arms and face, made her aware all over again of the aura of powerful masculinity he emanated. Thank heaven he couldn't read her thoughts.

'Lanie!' Lost in her thoughts, she blinked as his stern tones recalled her to her reason for being here.

'Sir!' She straightened and opened her eyes wide in mock alarm. 'Orders are——?'

He eyed her narrowly, that mesmeric gaze she found so difficult to sustain. 'You know what you have to do?'

She nodded. 'I've got a fair idea. At least, I've read all about it.'

'Read about it?' He bent on her his formidable stare. 'This is for real, and you'd better pay attention!'

'Sir!'

He refused to be amused. He was wearing his familiar 'must-keep-young-Lanie-under-control' look, she reflected as he went on in the inexorable tones he seemed to keep just for her. 'For starters, you'll need this——' Striding away, he returned a few moments later with a straw broom. 'When I've freed the fleece and released the ewe then you move in with your broom to clear the stand and take the fleeces over to the sorting table. Dags, bellies and pieces all go into separate piles—I'll show you how it goes with the first lot and after that it's over to you—think you can handle it?'

Lanie wrinkled her nose at him. 'It looks as if I'll have to,' she told him with spirit.

'That's my—the idea!' She could have sworn he had been about to say 'that's my girl' and had hurriedly changed the words. The suspicion went to her head and all at once she felt confident of carrying out the unfamiliar tasks.

'It's a bit different today from when the gangs are in action,' she brought her mind back to his tones, 'then the pace is always on, but all the same it's the team spirit that counts. It's a matter of timing and working together.' He bent on her one of his swift penetrating glances. 'You did say you'd have a go at anything?'

'It's good experience, I think,' she declared warmly, 'being part of a team. Especially,' she couldn't resist the opportunity of getting something of her own back, 'when it's a man-and-woman team!'

The moment the words left her lips she knew she had gone too far. For something leaped in his eyes, kindling flames he couldn't hide from her gaze, and she knew it was only with an effort he was restraining himself from physical retaliation. A kiss, another kiss in the intimacy of the shadowy surroundings—was that what he imagined she was angling for? At the thought she felt her cheeks flame and hurriedly she averted her face.

He said tautly, 'You'd better give me a hand to get sheep into the pen.' She was only too glad to do as he said.

Before long Jard was bent over a ewe, one hand holding the animal while with the other he sheared away the heavy fleece. As Lanie watched his expert movements she realised why shearing was regarded as the hardest seasonal farm chore, depending on the shearer's physical strength combined with a co-ordination of eye and hand. Intent on watching his rippling muscles under the mahogany tanned skin, it was only as the fleece fell to the slippery floor that she recalled her own job of work in the team. A man-and-woman team with a difference, she thought wryly, and began to pick up fleeces and carry the armfuls of soft wool to a long table. Soon she was sorting out the wool for impurities as he had shown her. Before she had made much headway, however, it was time to clear the stand, and she picked up the straw broom and swept away the scraps of wool from the littered floor, while Jard went to the back door to bring another sheep to the stand.

It was a pattern of work repeated again and again. As the hours wore on the sun mounted in a cloudless sky, its rays beating down on the iron-roofed shed. Now Lanie's white shirt, sleeves rolled above her elbows, was streaked with dust, her forehead beaded with perspiration, and in her nostrils was the musky smell of sheep under strain. Now there was no opportunity for talk or for anything else, for that matter. Jard worked hard and fast, maintaining a smooth steady pace and somehow it had become very important for her to keep up with him.

Head bent over the sorting table, she classed the fleeces as best she could, hoping feverishly that she wasn't making any frightful blunders, for if so she would hear about them from Jard, no doubt about that!

'Smoko!' The cry rang through the shed and Jard, returning after releasing a sheep in the pen outside, strode forward.

'Am I welcome or aren't I?' called a cheerful masculine voice, and Lanie paused in her task. Wiping a hand over her wet forehead, she met Mervyn's grin.

'Are you ever!' Lanie didn't know when she had been so glad to see anyone. 'If I wasn't such a mess, I'd throw my arms around your neck to thank you, I'm so glad to have a break!' She perched on the table, swinging a bare foot, for she had long since kicked off her rubber thongs.

'I don't mind about your being a mess——' Grinning, he set down on the table a wooden tray with a long handle, then placed beside the tray a billy of tea. 'You look fine to me! Hi,' he called as Jard returned from the side door where he had released a newly-shorn sheep, and came to join them. 'Your lady cook roped me on this job,' he explained cheerfully, 'told me if I was just going to hang around the house all day waiting for the sheep to be shorn and something else,' he threw Lanie a laughing glance, 'but I won't go into that. I might as well make myself useful.' He was pouring steaming tea into cups and handing one to Lanie. 'Your Edna isn't the sort of woman one argues with. Seems I've got myself a job in the catering department!' His warm glance went to Lanie, her face flushed and hot from the soaring temperatures of the shed and tendrils of red-gold hair lying damply against her forehead. 'Not that I'm complaining—just hoping that if I stick around long enough——' He had a pleasant way of speaking, Lanie thought, slow and sort of smiling.

'Make it quick, Lanie!' Jard's terse tones cut across the lazy accents. 'We haven't got all day.'

She took a gulp of hot tea that burned her lips. The sudden harshness of Jard's tone took her by surprise, and even Mervyn appeared somewhat taken aback. Had she not known Jard to be incapable of such an emotion concerning his new shed-hand, almost she could have imagined he was displaying jealousy, just as he was in the habit of doing with dear old Sandy. Sandy, of all men! It was absurd, of course—she shook the thought away. He was the big boss of Rangimarie and accustomed to ordering people around to suit himself, darn him! The maddening thing was that in situations such as this he happened to be in the right. All the same, she mused resentfully, he had no reason to look so stern and somehow ... angry. Mervyn hadn't done a thing to merit Jard's displeasure, except to pay her some attention.

Soon, however, Mervyn had picked up the box with the empty cups and left the shed, and there was no time to think of anything except the matter in hand.

In the heat and hurry-up of the shearing shed, it

seemed to Lanie to be no time at all before Mervyn was back once more, his tray loaded with freshly baked scones—scones that were soft and fluffy. Why hadn't her baking efforts ever turned out like this? The lunch box contained as well a pizza pie and, surprisingly, small apple pies. Lanie breathed a sigh of relief. So she hadn't after all sneaked all Edna's hoard in the deep freeze. Or had the cook tossed off a fresh batch of apple pies?

On this occasion Mervyn left the tray and turned away with a few words tossed over his shoulder. 'See you up at the house, Lanie.' Small wonder he wasn't disposed to linger, she thought, seeing that Jard had shown no particular pleasure in his company. How annoying could a man get?

She straightened her back and began to pour out the tea, then, cup in hand, she dropped down to seat herself on a filled wool bale. Amazingly, she reflected, Jard didn't appear to be at all weary. But then he wouldn't be tired, he was supremely fit, anyone could see it. He would need to be in order to carry out his duties on the station. For something to say she asked, 'How long do you think we'll take to get through the lot?'

He threw her a quizzical glance. 'Want to chicken out?'

'*No!*' she protested with such vehemence that he gazed at her in surprise, then raised his brows.

'Okay, okay, I was only asking.' After a minute he ran on, 'We had sixty-five sheep all told and we've saved time with your not having to take the car up to the house for smokos. Another couple of hours should do it. Then you can run your straw broom over the floor and call it a day.'

He was certainly a tiger for work, she reflected a short while later as he got to his feet purposefully. 'All set to get going again?'

'Right!' She stacked the cups and plates on the tray, then turned away to pick up her broom. As she eyed the piles of separated fleeces lying on the sorting table she comforted herself with the thought that at least she

could see something for her hours of gruelling toil in
the enervating heat of the shed.

Presently she was once more bending over the table,
laboriously sorting the fleeces into separate piles,
unconscious of the hours flying by.

'How's it going?'

In his soft rubber jandals, she hadn't heard him
approach, and now he was at her side, towering above
her, leaning over her shoulder as he fingered a pile of
fleeces. His nearness sent her senses spinning. What was
it about him, she wondered wildly, that affected her so?
It wasn't as if she even liked the man, anything but! The
thought spurred her to pull herself back to sanity.

'I'm not exactly speedy!' She glanced upwards and
under the impact of his gaze the tingling awareness was
pulsing through her veins. 'If this is the clean pile for
carpet wool,' she chattered wildly, scarcely aware of
what she was saying, 'I'll never again think carpets are
expensive . . . all this work!'

'You're doing fine.' He was still running his fingers
through the fleeces.

Ridiculous how the few words of praise sent the
warmth surging through her. 'Not a bad team in the
shearing shed——' He was having a joke at her
expense, throwing off at her lack of expertise of course,
he always was. And yet——

A swift upward glance gave her the answer, for she
surprised a look, almost a tenderness that made her
heart plunge. His slow words seemed to her to be
measured out in heartbeats. 'You and me.'

She wrenched her spinning senses back to his vibrant
tones. 'I'd give you a job in the shed as rouseabout any
time!' His tone was entirely matter-of-fact. She *must*
have imagined the look of tenderness in his gaze.

She had no idea how much later it was when Jard
stood upright, wiping his wet brow with a handkerchief.
'Right, that's it! Want to come and see this one take
off?'

'Love to.' She went with him as he released the
freshly shorn sheep from the pen. Lanie laughed,

watching the animal leap high in the air and land on the grass below. 'At least he'll feel a lot more comfortable now. Imagine wearing a woolly coat in this heat!'

'Feeling it, are you?'

Just for a moment, she thought, he had evidently forgotten who she *really* was. Right now she was only his rouseabout. 'A bit,' she admitted, 'but a cool shower and some clean clothes will soon put me right.'

Jard baled the wool while she swept up the last fragments of fleece from the floor and soon they were moving out of the doors together. To all appearances, she mused, they were just a man and a girl who had completed satisfactorily a job they had done together. Togetherness, her mouth curved wryly at the thought, was scarcely the word she would use when describing the relationship that existed between the boss and herself. At least, not if he had any say in the matter. With her it was different—— She caught herself up sharply. Now where in the world could that errant thought have come from?

Outside in the dazzling sunlight, the surf was pounding in on the glittering black sands and rugged bays stretched away in the distance in a mist of surf-spray. Jard flung open the door of the dust-smeared car and she slid inside, throwing back her head to feel on her flushed face the touch of the salty fresh breeze. He took the wheel, spinning the car around on ground where sand mingled with springy grass, then they were taking the worn track running beside the beach and turning up sheep-threaded slopes. As they sped towards the homestead, Lanie felt an odd contentment. Probably, she told herself sceptically, it was due to having stopped work in the blistering heat of the iron-roofed shed. It *couldn't* be anything to do with being here with Jard. Still, she conceded dreamily, he had an attractive voice, a 'dark brown voice', and there were rare occasions when he actually seemed to approve of her. Like that moment in the shed—or had she merely imagined the softened expression in his gaze? She wrenched her mind back to the vibrant tones. 'The last girl we had working in the shed happened to be one of a shearing gang. She was rouseabout too, a very ambitious girl, Beverley.'

'Ambitious?'

'She had hopes of being one of the few women shearers in the country, and the only way she could get in any practice with the shears was to have a learner's lesson before afternoon shearing started.'

'You mean she had no midday break?' Lanie marvelled. 'No lunch hour either? My goodness, she must have been keen to learn how to shear!'

Jard grinned, sending her a sideways glance as they moved up the sandy track. 'Not for you, I take it?'

'Definitely not!' She pulled a face. 'I'd have had enough of the shed by lunchtime to need a break!'

But if you were there with me, just the two of us alone in the shed, I'd stay there all day long. I wouldn't mind the heat and the dust and the hard, hard work. The thought came unbidden and she thrust it aside.

When they reached the house she went straight to her own room, thankful for the bathroom at her disposal. The shower of warm water followed by fluffy towels and perfumed talc dispelled the dirt and dust and perspiration of the hours spent in the shed. A little later, clad in fresh undergarments, she thrust a white T-shirt over her head, pulled on newly-laundered denim jeans and combed into place the waves of springy, damp hair.

In the sun-splashed lounge room, Mervyn was waiting for her.

'Wow-ee!' He got to his feet, eyeing her appreciatively. 'I've got to be on my way, but I had to see you before I took off, something important that I wanted to ask you about, at least it's important to me!' His gaze took in Lanie's round, dimpled face. 'Where's the rouseabout girl now?'

She laughed. 'It wasn't too bad. I don't even feel tired—well, not all that much.'

'You don't look it——' Unexpectedly he leaned forward and dropped a kiss on the tip of her blunt little nose. 'Your fault, you look good enough to eat!'

She mocked lightly, 'Wet hair and all?'

He put out a hand to lift a long damp strand falling past her shoulders. 'I like your hair this way,' he said softly.

For something to say, she asked, 'Have you come far to bring the sheep over here?'

'Not too far.' His warm gaze lingered on Lanie's young face. 'I wouldn't have missed this trip for anything!' His dark eyes said: Now that I've met you. 'It's not every day of the week that you come across a girl who's a——'

'City rouseabout,' she put in laughingly. 'Come on now, admit it. Wasn't that what you were going to say?'

'Not exactly. If they all look like you——' His words trailed into silence and she realised that Jard had come into the room. Freshly showered, his dark blond hair as damp as her own red-gold locks, he had changed levis for green corduroy slacks and a short-sleeved cream knit shirt replaced the black bush shirt he had worn in the shed. There was a magic about him, she mused, so that just seeing him come into the room made life all at once seem more exciting. With an effort she wrenched her mind back to Mervyn. 'I wasn't very expert at the job,' she admitted. 'Next time I'll be quicker with the broom and sorting out the fleeces.'

At that moment she glanced up to meet Jard's smile. It was a reluctant, twisted sort of smile, she realised, but still . . . He said, 'You were okay, Lanie, got along fine!'

Faint praise. She couldn't understand the joy that was singing along her nerves or why she was feeling this sudden happiness, as if she were treading on air.

Jard had moved to the cocktail cabinet and releasing the tab of a can of chilled beer, he poured a glass and handed it to Mervyn. 'How about you, Lanie? A chilled orange juice? You've earned it.'

'Thank you.' She took the glass he offered her, then flicked him a challenging glance from under her eyelashes. 'Tell me, what have you got lined up for me in the way of work tomorrow?'

'Tomorrow?' He straddled a chair and eyed her enquiringly and once again she had difficulty in meeting his deep, compelling gaze. 'What would you like to do?'

What would she *like*? The words were so un-Jardlike that once again she wondered if he were thinking of her as just the rouseabout girl, any rouseabout girl. Before he could revert to his usual disapproving attitude she answered promptly, 'Riding for me! If you've got anything offering in that line I'd love it!'

'How about taking a ride over the paddocks and checking if the creeks in the gully aren't too dry? Can do?'

'Oh *yes*, that would be fine!'

'What's all this?' Mervyn's pleasant face wore an expression of astonishment. 'I got the idea you were a townie born and bred, Lanie?'

'She's a good rider.' Could this really be Jard's voice she was hearing? The next moment he spoiled it all by sending her a quizzical glance. 'Even if she does have to bale out on the odd occasion!'

'That was because of the bush fire you started up on the hill,' she protested hotly.

'True, true.' He appeared to have lost interest in her riding prowess. 'I'll get one of the boys to saddle up one of the station hacks in the morning,' he murmured. It was as easy as that. Lanie couldn't believe her luck.

Jard took a draught of beer, then eyed Mervyn speculatively. 'How are things in the big city?'

'Much the same as usual. You know something?' Thoughtfully Mervyn studied his glass. 'I've been kicking an idea around for quite a while now. I've half a mind to give the city life away and take my chances on a farm job. Uncle Ned's put it to me that if I get myself some training in sheep farming, he'll put me on here to manage the place for him. Today, for instance, I could have shorn those sheep instead of giving you the job.'

Jard's voice was ironic. 'There's a bit more to it than that. If you're really interested in this way of life, it might pay you to join up with a shearing gang for a couple of seasons and get the know-how——'

Lanie sipped her chilled drink. 'If you can survive a week in the shearing shed,' she told him laughingly, 'you can endure anything!'

'That's the crunch,' Mervyn's tone was thoughtful, 'but I'm coming around to thinking it could be worthwhile.'

Something tugged at her mind. 'What was it,' she asked curiously, 'that you wanted to tell me?'

'Oh, that' he shot an uneasy glance towards Jard. Was Mervyn hoping that the other man would leave the room and he could speak with her in private? If so, she mused wryly, Mervyn was going to be out of luck, for Jard, staring out of the window, showed no indication of moving away. Standing tall and erect, he was gazing out over sheep-threaded slopes. She thought he looked indominable and very much the master of his vast domain. 'Thing is,' Mervyn dropped his voice, 'one of the neighbours is putting on a dance in the woolshed tomorrow night. There'll be quite a crowd turning up, from what I hear on the grapevine.'

Suddenly Lanie wasn't feeling the least bit weary any more. She glanced up at him eagerly, 'sounds like fun!'

His grin was wide and heart-warming, as if, she thought in some surprise, it really mattered to him whether or not a strange girl accompanied him to a back-country dance to be held in a farmer's woolshed. 'Just as well,' she teased, 'that I cleaned myself up a bit today or I might not have been asked to go along with you!'

'You looked great to me,' his tone softened, 'even with fleece in your hair and bare feet——' He broke off, and she became aware that he too had caught the mocking twist to Jard's lips. Clearly a little rattled by Jard's satirical gaze, he ran on quickly, 'They don't get into gear until after nine. I've been there before, so I know the ropes. How about if I pick you up at eight? It's a fair step over there as the crow flies or the uncle's Land Rover bumps along the hill tracks.'

'Sorry, mate,' Lanie thought that Jard's tight

expression was anything but apologetic, 'but Lanie'll be coming along with the rest of the party from here.'

Disappointment was written all over Mervyn's downcast face. 'But I thought——'

'It's all taken care of!' Jard's peremptory tones cut him short. 'There are quite a few going from here.' He tossed off his drink. 'The new stockman can't wait to take his guitar along to the woolshed hop and the girls in the cottages have threatened their husbands that they'll leave home if they don't get taken along tomorrow night. Around here,' he tossed the words towards Lanie' 'social life isn't what you'd call hectic, and those two girls are determined they're not going to miss out on the fun!'

'Actually I wanted——' Mervyn's effort to maintain his side of the argument was neatly sidestepped by Jard. 'Like I said, that's the way things work out around here.' He was as cool and authoritative and maddening, Lanie thought vexedly, as only he knew how to be. She could have told Mervyn that he was wasting his time in attempting to go against Jard's wishes. That when it was a matter concerning a member of his staff, Jard held the reins firmly in control. Didn't she know it! She was feeling as resentful of the boss's overbearing attitude as Mervyn obviously was, and she made a mental vow that she would have it out with Jard at her first opportunity, but not while Mervyn was here.

Evidently, however, Mervyn hadn't yet given up the argument. He said firmly, 'Anyway, I'll come over and get you, Lanie.'

Before she could make an answer Jard's satirical tones cut in. 'I wouldn't bother if I were you.' And somehow she felt that he meant business. 'I'll give you a hand to get those ewes back in the truck!'

Lanie glared at him. Well, really! Of all the nerve! What right had he to interfere in Mervyn's arrangements, she thought vexedly. It was none of Jard's business and she would tell him so too when he came back from seeing Mervyn off in the truck. All at once she became aware of Mervyn's low tones. 'Goodbye,

Lanie, see you tomorrow night.' Catching Jard's eye, he added resignedly, 'At the woolshed.' He lifted his hand in a gesture of farewell and because she knew that Jard was watching, she put on her brightest smile and blew him a kiss.

She watched from the window as the two men loaded the stock into the truck and when Jard returned to the room, she flung around to face him, eyes glinting with anger. 'Why,' she demanded, 'did you stop Mervyn from coming to collect me to go to that dance?' A sudden thought spun through her mind. 'You don't mind my going there, do you?'

'Mind?' He bent on her his cold forbidding stare. 'Why should I mind? Since you're asking, I would have imagined that Sandy could put you right on that one.'

'Sandy?' Bewilderment clouded her gaze. 'What has he got to——'

'Forget it!' He stopped her with his hard tone. 'Put it this way, all I'm doing is helping your young man to save his petrol.'

'He's *not* my young man!' she returned fiercely.

'Well then, it doesn't matter, does it?' he suggested with deceptive gentleness. 'Just get one thing straight— I'll be taking you to that show tomorrow night.'

She eyed him incredulously. 'You will?'

'Why not? When anyone in the district puts on a woolshed dance, everyone for miles around is welcome there, and that includes Mum, Dad and the kids.' *So don't get any mistaken notions into your head about my having any personal feelings in the matter.* Is that what you're trying to get through to me, boss?

Sticking to her guns in spite of everything, she said doggedly, 'But he was coming to pick me up.' Somehow now that she had put the thought into words, it seemed a trivial matter to be arguing about. Nevertheless. . . .

'No need.' He simply wiped the suggestion. 'He'd have been wasting his time and his petrol!'

So, Lanie thought resentfully, he had succeeded in defeating her just as he had talked Mervyn into accepting his orders. The master of Rangimarie had spoken, she thought ruefully, and taking in the hard unyielding lines of his face, she didn't see how she could alter the arrangements. She said coldly, 'I really don't mind about going to the dance. I mean, please don't put yourself out on my account.'

'No trouble.' For a timeless moment his gaze meshed in hers and once again those twin flames kindled in his eyes. With an effort she wrenched her glance aside and brought her mind back to his dispassionate tones. 'I was going along anyway.'

Humiliation washed over her, and with it came a hot tide of anger. Never ever, she told herself with heightened colour, had she hated anyone as she hated this man! 'Please, *please*,' she offered up a prayer, 'let him ask me to dance with him, just once would do, so that I can turn him down flat!'

CHAPTER EIGHT

Next day she awoke early and soon she was strolling out into the early morning air, fresh with the salty tang of the sea. All around her she was aware of colour and life and movement. How anyone could find station life lonely, she mused, was something she would never understand.

As she neared the stables she caught sight of Brent's lanky frame as he led a station hack down the green slope nearby and she hurried to meet him, the sun turning her red-gold hair to flame.

His eyes softened with pleasure at sight of Lanie's slim young figure and alive expression, but she was aware only of the mount he was leading. She patted the mare's sturdy neck. 'Can't wait to get going! Tell me, what's her name?'

'Trixie, and they tell me she's just the one for you. No hang-ups over a bush fire, steady as a rock no matter what!'

She pulled a face at him.

'Not to worry,' he assured her, 'she can travel if you want her to. Want me to give you a demo?'

Her laughing gaze challenged him. 'You're on!'

'Right!' He threw the bridle over the mare's head, sprang into the saddle and guided the mount towards the flat below. Then, leaning forward in the saddle, he urged her on until the flying hooves were at full gallop and horse and rider seemed to merge into one.

A hand shielding her eyes against the sun-glare, Lanie watched as Brent dropped the mare to a walk, then reaching Lanie's side, he dropped lightly down to the dried grass. 'Well, what do you think? Will she do?'

'Will she ever!' Lanie stroked the bay mare's velvety nose.

'Right!' He gave her a leg up into the saddle. 'Jard

told me to give you a message. Seems he wants you to go over the ridge over that away,' he waved a hand in the direction of a sun-dried slope, 'and check on the dams down in the gully. Orders are you have to call it a day at midday.'

'Oh?' She drew rein, surprised at the words. 'I wonder why midday?'

He grinned. 'You'll soon know after you've spent a few hours in the saddle in the heat! See you!' He stood watching her as she turned her mount and rode away.

Hours later, when the sun was high in the blue translucent bowl of the sky, Lanie had to admit that maybe, just maybe, there had been good sense in Jard's advice. She had been riding for miles following the course of a creek deep in a green gully, and now had to admit to a longing she had had for quite a time, to return to the homestead.

When she reached the house she showered, changed her shirt and jeans, and went into the dining room where the others were seated around the table. Jard, entering the room at the same moment, sent her an assessing glance. 'How are you feeling, Lanie?'

She was aching in every limb, but she forced a carefree smile, at least she hoped it looked carefree. 'Never better!'

He eyed her with his penetrating glance. 'All the same, you wouldn't say no to a free afternoon?'

'Oh *no*!' Her expression of relief betrayed her feelings.

Everyone laughed, including the big boss himself. It was Sandy who pulled out a chair for her and said warmly, 'You've done a good job, by the sound of things.'

'Has she?' Jard's cold tones cut in. She met his familiar cool glance. 'How was the creek? Water dried up in any of the shallow spots!'

He made her so angry! Was he deliberately baiting her? Clearly he still distrusted her, believing her to be incapable of doing a job properly. The thought sparked her to spring to her feet. She lifted her rounded chin and sent him a smart salute. 'Reporting all stock

accounted for—creek water all present and correct—
sir!' Amidst the gale of laughter echoing around her she
dropped back to her seat.

Edna was laughing so heartily she had to wipe her
streaming eyes with her apron, the one Lanie had worn
throughout her brief period as cook. She recognised it
by the many burn holes, although the grease marks had
been washed away. 'I really don't know what we'd do
without you, Lanie,' Edna said affectionately. 'You
certainly brighten up the day!'

Lanie didn't answer. She was stealing a glance from
under her eyelashes at Jard. His face was set and
unsmiling and it was clear that she didn't brighten up
the boss's day one little bit!

Late in the afternoon, feeling surprisingly refreshed
after the break, she decided to take a stroll down to a
part of the station she hadn't yet explored where she
had noticed the neatly painted white timber cottages
occupied by the two young shepherds and their families.
The men she had met briefly, but she hadn't yet made
the acquaintance of their wives, and this seemed a good
time to do something about it.

Long before she came in sight of the stockyards she
caught the lowing of cattle, and presently she
recognised Jard's tall sinewy frame in the dust of the
yards. He was busy ear-tagging steers and appeared not
to notice her wave of greeting. She was conscious of an
odd sense of disappointment. Come to think of it, she
mused, for one reason or another he was a lot in her
thoughts. She found herself dwelling on him—well,
most of the time, her gaze seeking his erect figure as he
rode past the homestead on his white horse Snow. Or
searching the dusk for his return at the end of his day's
work. Evenings too ... strange how empty the lounge
seemed to her when he had left the room to catch up
with paper work in his office or to go to the billiard
room up the hall with Sandy.

Jard ... her random steps took her far along the
winding path, but she was unaware of her surroundings.
Always about him she sensed an air of aloofness that

she never seemed able to penetrate, yet somehow he fascinated her. Could it be because she both hated and—she brought her thoughts up with a jerk, appalled at the direction in which they were leading. Absurd, she chided herself. They had known each other for so brief a time. But what has time to do with love? a voice queried deep in her mind. Like it or not, she had to admit that he strode endlessly through her dreams, she couldn't get him out of her mind. His hard-muscled body and supple strength, his moments of unexpected tenderness. What would it be like, the thought came unbidden, to be loved by a man of Jard's calibre? But of course, unconsciously she sighed, he had his Paula. Paula, who was such a fitting match for him. She had every attribute he could want in a girl. Beauty, sophistication, similar interests and there seemed little doubt but that she was crazy about him. Fool, she scolded herself, he's way out of your reach! Forget him. If only she could.

Absorbed in her thoughts as she was, it was with a shock of surprise that she realised her steps had brought her to a neat paling fence enclosing a white painted cottage. She must put Jard out of her mind and concentrate on other matters or she was lost indeed. She pressed a finger to the doorbell, but although she heard it jangling inside the house, there was no answer to the summons and at length she wandered down a flower-bordered path to the rear of the dwelling. Two young women wearing colourful sun-frocks were seated on the springy green grass while a toddler, vigorously banging pot lids, was seated between them.

'I know you!' A fair-haired girl, extremely slim with a sensitive face, got to her feet. 'It's Elaine, from the house isn't it? I'm Debbie. Take a seat.' She pulled forward a canvas chair.

Lanie smiled, 'That's me.' Ignoring the chair, she dropped down to the clipped lawn grass. 'What an adorable little boy. Is he yours?'

'Oh yes,' said Debbie, 'he's mine, and Rob's. Do you know Rob? See one, you see the other.'

'I've met him, just for a minute.'

'Oh, sorry, Mary,' Debbie turned to her friend, 'this is Elaine.'

'We've been dying to meet you.' She was a short girl, rather plain in appearance, with short-cropped black hair. 'We've been looking forward to seeing you at the dance tonight.'

'You're going?'

'Hope so. That's why we've got our hair in rollers. We're getting ready for a night out. It all depends on Clara. She's promised to baby sit for Debbie, but she might just get one of her headaches on the wrong night. Anyway, we're keeping our fingers crossed!'

Both girls were eyeing Lanie with interest and she guessed that the company of young women of their own age didn't often come their way. 'Don't tell me,' she laughed, reaching out a hand to clasp the plump fingers of the small boy, who was taking an unsteady step towards her, 'I know what you're going to say! What are you going to wear?'

The words came in unison and ended up in laughter. The next moment the child, after an uncertain glance towards his young mother, joined in the merriment.

'It's not really a problem with me,' Lanie explained, 'seeing I have only one dance frock—and I only hope,' she added doubtfully, 'that it won't look too dressed up for a country hop. It's one of those sheer dresses, pale grey with a pleated shirt.'

'I know what you mean.' Debbie's voice held a wistful note. 'They're all the rage in town, judging by the fashion ads in the newspapers. Oh well, I guess our old faithfuls will have to see us through for one more time!'

'The main thing,' Mary comforted her briskly, 'is being there. I'll go up the wall before long if I don't get some social life!'

'Should be fun.' Thoughtfully Lanie pulled at a long blade of grass as she tried to find the right words to frame the question that trembled on her lips. 'Do the others up at the house go to the woolshed do's?'

'Edna and Clara used to,' it was Mary who answered the query. 'Just to look on and meet everyone there, but they haven't bothered lately. Sandy doesn't dance, he told me once he's always regretted not having learned the know-how, and Jard——'

Lanie found she was holding her breath for the next words. 'He only goes along if he takes Paula with him,' Debbie said lightly.' I guess those two are so used to each other's steps they wouldn't even know they were dancing! Paula usually comes here early in the day when something's on at night. It's funny,' she added thoughtfully, 'that she hasn't arrived already.'

'I know she's home again, came back yesterday.' Mary's tones seem to have some hidden implication. 'I can't imagine Jard going to the dance without her. And any of the other guys here could see to the transport. It's very strange.'

Debbie said, smiling, 'Maybe he's taking an interest in some other girl—at last.'

'Or Paula turned him down?'

'Are you joking? She'd never do that!'

Lanie couldn't help feeling a sneaky sense of relief when the toddler fell to the grass and his loud cries of anguish brought the conversation to an end.

Presently Debbie went into the house, to return with a tray holding steaming mugs of coffee, and soon both girls were plying Lanie with tales of the station and the endlessly enthralling matters concerning the change of seasons and work and stock, and the friends they termed 'neighbours', though they lived in homesteads scattered far over the hills.

Later, as she strolled back along the winding track, she mused how strange it was that the two young wives, just like the men who worked for Jard, appeared to share this feeling that he was someone special, a man of substance and authority who was thoughtful and considerate to those who were associated with him, a runholder noted for his fair dealing. She gathered the impression that to be in Jard's employ was sufficient to guarantee a shepherd or stockman a worthwhile job on any one of the great stations throughout the country. It seemed that Jard's name held a special sort of magic for everyone at Rangimarie. *Just as it does you?* She thrust the ridiculous thought aside.

That evening Lanie found herself taking particular pains with her appearance. It was fun to be getting ready for a dance, to dress up a little and change from jeans and T-shirt that had become a standard wear for her nowadays. Tonight, preferring a natural look, she left her complexion clear and made up her eyes with blue-grey shadow and mascara. Then, studying her reflection in the mirror, she pulled her bright hair back from her face and twisted it high in a topknot. There! At least she looked a little more dignified, a trifle older, if not all that sophisticated, she decided with some satisfaction. Sophistication, however, made her remember Paula and somehow the thought of the other girl was definitely depressing. She couldn't think why. Could it be, the thought came unbidden, because Jard seemed wrapped up in Paula? She thrust the ridiculous supposition aside and concentrated on her dress, pulling over her head the diaphanous drift of misty grey, its soft folds falling in just the right places to accentuate her petite figure.

She fastened tiny silver earrings in her ears and slipped her feet into high-heeled silver sandals. Then as an afterthought she pinned to her shoulder the pink, perfumed silk rose that by some lucky chance she had packed in her travel bag.

The loud tooting of car horns brought her to the window, and she peered into the gathering darkness where two cars were sweeping past the homestead entrance. Probably, she mused, the vehicles would take care of the transport for the married shepherds and their wives together with the stockmen employed on the station. If so then she would be driven to her destination by the big boss himself! The prospect was disturbing, and she only hoped that Edna had had second thoughts about giving the social evening a miss tonight in favour of her favourite television programme.

It was a forlorn hope she realised the moment she

went into the lounge room, for Clara had already left the house on her babysitting stint while Edna, her knitting lying on her ample lap, was gazing fixedly towards the small screen. At that moment, however, she caught sight of Lanie, looking sweet and fresh and glowingly attractive. 'You look lovely, pet!'

'It's not really me,' Lanie disclaimed modestly, 'it's the dress.'

'Rubbish!' Sandy had come to join them, his twinkling gaze resting on Lanie's young face. 'You're a sight for sore eyes tonight, lass, and no mistake!'

She was scarcely aware of his words, for Jard had come into the room. The bush shirt and denim jeans he had worn during the day had been replaced by immaculate fawn slacks and a fine cream polo-necked sweater. Freshly shaven, his thatch of tawny hair was brushed sleekly down over his sun-tanned forehead and he looked, Lanie had to admit to herself, extremely attractive—even with the cold unyielding look in his eyes that he seemed to keep just for her!

'Looks a picture, doesn't she?' Sandy jerked his head towards Lanie. 'Don't you agree?' His smiling gaze challenged his son.

Lanie held her breath for the answer. She was all too aware of Jard's veiled glance flickering over her face with obvious lack of interest. Trust him not to answer that one, she thought ruefully, and brought her mind back to the curt tones. 'Sure, sure—let's get going, shall we?'

She tried not to let the disappointment show. The brief moments of pleasure the compliments on her appearance had brought her, died away and instead came the familiar sense of conflict. Had she really expected Jard to hand out flattering comments about her? She must have been out of her mind to even think of such a thing! None of her chagrin, however, showed in her face as she bade Sandy and Edna goodbye.

'Don't they make a perfect couple, those two?' Edna's sentimental tones reached them clearly as they went out of the door. 'He's so tall, and she barely reaches up to his shoulder——'

Lanie was about to make a joke of Edna's words, but glancing up into Jard's face with its hard, unyielding expression, she thought better of it.

Outside the Land Rover was parked at the foot of the steps and she climbed up the step and slid into the passenger seat. He closed the door behind her, swung his tall frame effortlessly into the cab and set the sturdy vehicle in motion. Soon they were clattering over the cattlestop and moving towards the first of the gates. Lanie knew all about gates and how it was the passenger's duty to open and close them behind the vehicle. Almost she was glad of an excuse to jump out of the Land Rover and climb in again. There was something about being seated close to Jard that was sending her senses rioting in confusion. It didn't help any that as they took the dusty track winding over the hills she was bumped and jostled, thrown against his hard muscular body as they traversed the darkening slopes. Clouds of dust caught in the headlamps of the vehicle indicated that other vehicles weren't far away, even though they were out of sight around the sharp, tree-shaded bends.

Then they turned off, taking a track down a dark hill, and as they swung around a curve she caught sight of the dark outlines of a homestead high on a hill and far below, at the roadside, a great timber shed where lights blazed from wide open doors. Already she could glimpse the vehicles that were parked haphazardly around the high steps leading to the woolshed. She broke the long silence to eye Jard enquiringly. 'We're almost there?'

He nodded. 'That's right.' His glance was on the winding road ahead and soon he had guided the vehicle down the slope and was easing the Land Rover in between a long stock transporter and a timber truck. Then he jumped down to open the passenger door and Lanie dropped lightly to the dried grass, already wet with dew.

'They're here!' A group of young people gathered

around them and in a gale of talk and laughter they all moved towards the lighted building ahead. As they crowded up the steps Lanie realised that her companions were the everyday staff employed on the station, yet how different they appeared tonight in their gala attire. Especially the two girls, Mary and Debbie, with their freshly washed hair and skilfully applied make-up that enhanced their tanned complexions and clear bright eyes. Brent she scarcely recognised, his lean and lanky figure resplendent in cowboy gear he had evidently donned in anticipation of giving a musical item tonight—red-and-white checked cotton shirt, a heavily fringed leather jerkin, hip-hugging jeans. 'Glad you made it,' he whispered to Lanie, then she was borne along with the rest of the party as they surged through the opening into the big shed.

At the entrance they were welcomed by their hosts, a big quietly-spoken man and his smiling, pleasant-faced wife. Almost at once Jard was waylaid by a group of tanned young men whom Lanie took to be local sheep farmers. Already there was a crowd of people in the woolshed and as the banter echoed around her, Lanie stood gazing about her, her sweeping gaze taking in the colourful scene. Presses and tables had been pushed back against the walls, disguising the 'woolshed' image, and trailing greenery of long fronds of *punga* fern and fragrant five-finger, plucked from the bush, festooned bare corners. Trails of fairy lights were strung from high rafters, and hay bales set at intervals around the edge of the dance floor took care of the seating.

Her glance took in the sprinkling of older men with their leathery skins and calloused hands. With them were their wives, middle-aged, smiling women who were chatting with friends and evidently enjoying one of the rare social occasions in the district. Children were sliding up and down the grease-slippery floor. For the rest, there seemed to be a preponderance of young men, sun-weathered, athletic-looking types who were no doubt employed around the area as farm workers, shepherds and stockmen. It seemed to Lanie that tonight everyone for miles around had come to the dance—except Paula.

'Tell me,' all at once she became aware of a feminine voice cutting across the buzz of talk and laughter echoing around the big shed, 'who is she? The girl in front of us with the Rangimarie crowd? Must be one of their visitors they have to stay for a week or so. I mean the one with the cute little face and the dimples.'

Lanie winced at the description of herself. And she with her topknot and all! She had hoped that pulling her hair severely back from her face would lend her some small degree of sophistication, but now . . . Was she never to grow away from that childish image?

'Didn't you know? But of course you've been away from here for a while.' Lanie was so irritated by what she had unwittingly overheard concerning herself that she was scarcely aware of a second feminine voice. Now the words carried clearly in her direction. 'She's the new temporary cook who's filling in at Rangimarie while Edna's away overseas.'

'*A cook?*' Voice number two was incredulous. 'A girl like that? You're having me on!'

'It's true! Jard and his dad brought her back with them from town.'

'Now that I can believe, but the other . . .' The voice changed to a wistful note. 'Fresh blood in the district! She'll have lots of partners tonight. Funny, she doesn't seem to have a boy-friend with her. She's so pretty too.'

Voice number one was avid, gossipy. 'But she did have a boy-friend when she arrived here, quite a serious relationship it was too. Paula happened to be right there at the homestead when it happened. She saw the whole thing and she told me all about it. Elaine, the girl's name is. Seems she was all set to be married to this city guy, they'd worked together at the same office and had known each other for ages. Then Elaine came to work here. She wanted employment on a big station, Paula told me, and she said the reason wasn't hard to find. Anyway, this fellow from town followed her down here almost right away, drove all through the night to get here, and guess what? She was quite beastly to him, Paula told me, after he'd come all that way just to see her. She told him right away that the wedding plans were off!'

The other voice sounded younger, more innocent, the words tinged with bewilderment. 'But why would she do that, all of a sudden? Just because of the new job?'

'Not the job, stupid! Can't you guess? The man! The wealthy guy who owns Rangimarie! Paula told me that anyone could see what her game was. Not that she wouldn't be wasting her time, of course, when Jard and Paula—well, you know what I mean!' The speakers moved out of earshot, but Lanie had already heard enough, more than enough. She felt sick. It had been bad enough to have had Trevor voicing those crazy insinuations about her coming here to work for purposes of her own, but Paula ... How could the other girl spread such lies about someone she didn't even know? A dismaying thought ran through her mind. Had others here tonight besides herself been aware of the carrying tones of the unknown speakers?

At that moment, through the tumult of her thoughts, she became aware that all heads were turning towards the entrance as Paula swept into the big shed, a stunning figure in her low-cut gown, its clinging folds accentuating her slim figure.

She was running across the intervening space to greet Jard. 'Darling,' she cried delightedly, 'you *came!*' Laughingly, she raised herself on tiptoe to twine her arms around his neck, then she kissed him full on the lips. There was a ripple of laughter from the onlookers and she swung around with a mischievous wink. 'I'll let you into a secret!' For no reason at all, Lanie felt her heart plunge. 'If I hadn't chanced to ring up Rangimarie a while ago and found that he'd already left for this dance, he wouldn't have got himself that kiss!' Lanie's heart steadied. 'He had no idea that I was back home after my last trip. Just one of those stupid misunderstandings,' she ran on, 'but everything's all right now.' Her smile, Lanie was forced to admit, was really something. 'Isn't that true, Jard?' Her voice was a caress. 'I'll——' the words trailed into silence and her glance froze as she caught sight of Lanie's small figure all but hidden among the crowd. The next minute she had recovered herself. 'Listen!' She was laughing up into Jard's face. 'They're playing our tune. Remember?' From the makeshift stage the musicians, a pianist and two young Maori guitar-players, had broken into a melody and the foot-tapping rhythm pulsed through the big shed. 'Let's start things moving, shall we?'

As Paula and Jard took the floor, a hush fell over the chattering crowd. Lanie, watching with the others, thought that Jard appeared relaxed and apparently unconscious of the intricate steps his feet were performing. Paula was following his lead. In her figure-hugging red dress with its long floating sleeves, she resembled, Lanie mused wistfully, a scarlet-winged butterfly. Paula's eyes were sparkling and clearly she was enjoying the adulation of the onlookers.

'Gee, I'm so sorry I'm late!' The low contrite masculine tones fell on her ears and she swung around to find Mervyn at her side. Something in the expression of his steadfast brown eyes, or maybe it was the warmth of his smile, eased a little the chill sense of let-down that had been with her since the moment when she had found herself to be an unwilling witness to the malicious rumours that Paula had circulated around the district concerning her. She became aware of Mervyn's remorseful tones. 'The old bus let me down, refused to co-operate about starting, tonight of all nights! Been waiting long?'

'Not long.' Lanie endeavoured to concentrate on her companion, but she couldn't seem to wrench her gaze from Jard and Paula who she could glimpse through the maze of swaying figures who had now joined them on the dance floor.

'I scarcely recognised you.' Mervyn's appreciative gaze swept Lanie's petite young figure and small dimpled face. 'Let's not waste time,' he suggested smilingly, and swept her on to the dance floor that was now a scintillating, moving mass of colour.

When at last the pianist lifted his hands from the keyboard, Lanie was flushed and breathless. Mervyn led her from the dance floor, then almost at once the music resumed its rhythmic beat and before she realised what was happening, she found herself whisked away by Brent.

'I didn't see you anywhere near,' she commented in surprise as they moved to the intoxicating tempo, 'where were you?'

'Waiting and hovering, hoping for a chance of a dance with you!' he grinned. 'I knew I wouldn't have a hope in hell if I didn't do something about it!'

Strangely enough, she mused some time later, as things turned out it was the truth. Whether because of the novelty of an unfamiliar face at the back-country dance or because tonight men far outnumbered the girls, she couldn't tell. She only knew that she was in such demand as a partner that before long even Mervyn's good-tempered face wore a baffled expression. 'Why,' he groaned, 'did I have to pick on the most popular girl in the place to want to dance with?' Before long, however, by circumventing two bronzed young farmers who were bearing down in Lanie's direction, he managed to approach her side in the nick of time.

It was only during the space between numbers from the band when Brent, carrying his guitar, mounted the makeshift stage, that she found time to catch her breath. 'You have to be tough to go to these country dances,' she told Mervyn laughingly. 'They seem to be non-stop.'

His dark eyes held a twinkle. 'Do you mind?'

She laughed. 'Not really.'

'Me neither, not when I'm with you!'

There was a sudden hush in the buzz of conversation echoing around the room as Brent plucked his guitar and his voice, the sort of voice, Lanie thought, that could do things to your heart, took up the melody.

'I am a shepherd
With the stars for company.'

There was a haunting quality in the ballad, Lanie thought. It told of the long silences of the bush, of the loneliness of months spent in the isolation of a hut in remote country, far from human habitation. Or could it be his voice that touched her, she wondered, as Brent sang to the tempo of his throbbing guitar.

There was a lively lilt to the melody and before long everyone was joining in the foot-tapping chorus. In response to enthusiastic applause, Brent sang again and again until at last he left the stage to the accompaniment of stamping and calling from the audience.

Soon couples gathered once more on the dance floor and Lanie's pattern of popularity as a partner was repeated all over again. It seemed, she thought with some amusement, that every unattached male in the woolshed tonight wished to compete for a dance with 'the new girl from Rangimarie'. Everyone, that was, her steps faltered and she missed a beat, except Jard. Although why she should want him to partner her was beyond her comprehension except, she mused, as a means of taking her revenge on him. It wasn't as if they even liked each other. Why should he care about her when, had the matter been left to him, he would not keep her for a day in his employ? Besides— unconsciously she sighed—he had his Paula. Paula who had partnered him for all but one of the numbers when he had appeared on the dance floor. Lanie knew, because she had been keeping count, just as a matter of interest of course she told herself. Unconsciously she lifted her rounded chin. Even if he should ask her to partner him on the dance floor at this late hour she would take great pleasure, she vowed silently, in turning him down. Not that she need have concerned herself, she thought wryly a long time later when the hours had fled by and it was almost dawn. Lanie's face was flushed with exertion and her topknot was all over the place when at last the musicians rose from their seats on the makeshift stage to announce the final dance of the evening.

From the other side of the shed Mervyn was striding purposefully in her direction, but at that moment a tall figure appeared at her side and a vibrant, peremptory, *familiar* voice said, 'Mine, I think!' Before she had time to catch her breath, let alone tell him exactly what she had in mind, she found herself caught up in his arms. It *would* be waltz music, she thought faintly, that was throbbing from the guitars—a romantic, old-fashioned waltz to the tempo of an old ballad, Beneath a Maori Moon. Then she lost sight of her surroundings in the wild sweetness that flooded her senses. Jard was holding her firmly and closely, their steps matching as perfectly as if they had danced together many times. He was a faultless dancer and her own feet seemed to have wings. The crescendo of excitement mounted inside her, the world around her fell away and there was only she and Jard together, together, enmeshed in a golden web of melody.

When at last the music died away, Lanie felt as though she were coming back from somewhere far away. Jard took her back to join the group from the homestead, and as the band struck up the rousing notes of Auld Lang Syne Lanie, still in her private dream, linked hands with someone, a moment later she realised it was Mervyn's hand she was clasping, then the loud and enthusiastic singing filled the air.

Still under the influence of that last waltz, Lanie joined in with the others. Then suddenly, across the room, she encountered Paula's baleful glance. The other girl's lips were compressed in an ugly line and there was such a torrent of hate directed towards her that Lanie came back to reality with a rush. The singing had come to a rousing finish and now the human chain was breaking up and farewells were being said. All at once she realised that Mervyn was tugging at her arm. 'I had to share you with the whole world tonight,' he complained. 'Tell me,' she caught the note of urgency in his tone, 'when can I see you again?'

'I don't know—soon, I guess,' she murmured vaguely, her attention concentrated on Jard and Paula. The other girl was clinging to his arm and smiling up into his face. What were they saying? Lanie wondered.

'What a pity that Jard had lumbered himself with the rouseabout girl tonight'?

The next moment she became aware that Jard was weaving his way through the crowd towards her, and she half expected him to suggest that she return with the rest of the staff who would soon be driving back to the homestead. Mervyn's urgent tones scarcely penetrated. 'Lanie, will you *listen* to me? There's a show on next Saturday at Hamoana, not too far away. I could take you.' Jard had been intercepted, she saw, by a noisy young man, but he was still bound in her direction. She scarcely realised what she was saying.

'Give me a ring tomorrow,' she told Mervyn abstractedly, 'I'll have to ask Jard——'

'On a weekend? For Pete's sake——' He broke off as Jard's tall figure bore down on them and with a low 'See you,' Mervyn moved away. Lanie scarely noticed his going.

'Lanie?'

'Yes?' She held her breath, oblivious of the crowd surging around them, aware only of Jard. This was the moment when he would tell her that he was taking Paula home and Lanie would need to make other transport arrangements.

'Ready to hit the road?' A hand laid on her arm, he was escorting her through the throng amid a chorus of goodbyes and parting quips, then they were outside where brilliant stars spangled the intense darkness of the night sky. Jard saw her seated in the Land Rover, then moved around the vehicle and slid into the driver's seat. 'This time we'll make sure we won't collect their dust!' he grinned, his teeth white in the dimness. Then he switched on the headlamps and she glimpsed the rest of the party from the homestead, who were climbing into their cars. The next moment he set the heavy vehicle in motion, deftly weaving a route between the lighted cars, trucks and Land Rovers, then with a swing of the steering wheel they were speeding up the dark track. Soon they were turning into the main road, the sharp turn sending her lurching against him. At that moment it happened all over again, the wild sweet elation of just being here alone with him. She couldn't help it, it was the way he affected her, and so long as he didn't guess the riot of feelings his nearness evoked in her she was safe.

Just then they swung around a hairpin bend in the opposite direction and once again she found herself thrown off balance. Before she could right herself he threw a steadying arm around her shoulders. Any driver would do the same, Lanie told herself over the wild confusion of her senses. She made an effort to shift back to her own side of the seat, but the strong pressure of his arm drew her closer and she let herself relax against his tough hard nearness that she found so difficult to resist. She caught his low chuckle. 'Its a bumpy ride, you can do with a helping hand!'

They sped on along tree-shadowed tracks, the arc of the headlamps sweeping over ferns and bush overhanging the roadside.

Once the brilliant orbs of a possum, trapped in the glare of the lights, flashed out of the darkness to disappear in a tangle of undergrowth. It was a silent drive, but it was a happy sort of silence, Lanie mused in deep content laced with excitement. She wished the drive could go on for ever while she nestled close to his heart, his arm thrown around her shoulders. And then she had to spoil it all. Stupid! Stupid! Why did she have to say to him, 'I guess it was a bit hard on you and Paula, your being lumbered with taking me home with you tonight'?

Now the silence was ominous, charged with emotion. 'Not at all,' he countered harshly. Chilled by his hard tone, she stole a glance upwards and even in the dim light of the dashboard she glimpsed the betraying anger in his tightened features. He was furious with her for daring to intrude on his personal life. She could have kicked herself for spoiling everything. Her restive movements as she attempted to free herself from his grasp only made his hold tighten, and at last she ceased to struggle against his confining arm. She lifted her head from his chest. 'Why *did* you bring me?' She said the first thing that came into her mind. 'I could easily have gone back with the others, or Mervyn?' There, it was out! The question that had niggled at the back of her mind since last night when he had insisted on escorting her to the woolshed dance.

'Why did I insist?' The cool cutting note in his voice warned her that had she been looking for compliments she was in for a disappointment. 'Because as you're in my employ,' he said flatly, 'I'm responsible for your welfare. Do you understand?'

'No, I don't!' Danger signals were flashing all around her but some devil of perversity drove her on. 'I'd have been quite all right with the others.'

'Better with me!'

'That's what you think!' she flung at him angrily, and now at last she was free of his confining arm. 'Anyway, Mervyn would have saved you the bother of being lumbered with me. I'd have been safe with him——'

'You reckon?' His laugh was brief and humourless. 'He's a great guy, Mervyn, and there's only one thing against him. He happens to have crashed up more cars than anyone else in the district, and that's when he's only around at holiday times!'

'I still don't see,' Lanie muttered resentfully, 'how it can worry you about what happens to me. I know,' she added in a low throbbing tone, 'how you feel about me——'

He must have caught the barely audible words. 'You don't know!' Something in the harsh tones warned her that once again he was furious with her for venturing into forbidden territory. With a turn of the steering wheel he sent the vehicle off the road and crashing through a low bush towards a cleared track among tall *manuka* trees. He switched off the headlamps of the Land Rover and turned towards her, his voice dangerously soft. 'Shall I show you?'

'Yes—no——' Even in the dim light of the dashboard she caught the deep soft look in his eyes. She was trembling, her thoughts in such confusion that she scarcely knew what she was saying. The next moment his head was bent over her and his arms were around her, *really* around her, then his mouth came down on hers in urgent pressure. All the stars outside seemed to whirl in space and fire coursed through her veins as a tide of happiness carried her away to an unfamiliar world of ecstasy. At last Jard raised his head, to run his hand down her soft cheek. 'Lanie . . .' His voice, deep and soft and husky with emotion, reached her as from a distance, then once again his seeking lips were on hers. She scarcely realised the ardent response with which she was meeting his kiss. When she came back to sanity she was trembling, the chaotic thoughts tumbling wildly through her mind. Could it be that despite all the mistaken notions he held about her, the magic that drew her to him in spite of himself was a two-way thing? That he had planned to be alone with her on the long journey through the night?

'We'd better get cracking.' His tone was unexpectedly matter-of-fact. 'That is, if we don't want to collect the other cars' dust all the way back.'

Lanie, however, was still held fast in her own private dream. Dazed, happy, excited, she was barely aware of his words. 'One thing,' she was speaking her thoughts aloud, 'you've put me right about why you insisted on taking me home tonight!'

'Have I?' He was reaching a hand towards the starter motor. At the irony of his tone Lanie felt a chill creep through her. With a shock of surprise she realised that he had himself well in hand—too well in hand! Could it be that he was already regretting his brief madness with his rouseabout girl? Her spirits plunged and she drew away from him. Had the caress that had shaken her world been for him a meaningless after-dance gesture? A boss's kiss that an employee such as herself should understand? They were turning into the main road, but Lanie, absorbed in her thoughts, was scarcely aware of her surroundings. Fool, she chastised herself in distress, to have let herself imagine for one moment that there had been any real feeling in Jard's caress. Why hadn't she realised that his brief moments of tenderness had been no more than a passing physical attraction, what else? Maybe he had even liked her a little—at the time.

'Thing is,' his impassive tones underlined her heavy thoughts, 'I can't afford to risk anything happening to you. Not,' his harsh laugh was like a slap in the face, 'when I'd have to face my old man with the bad news!'

She felt a crashing sense of disappointment, but somehow she schooled her voice to a careless note. 'I get it.'

They continued the journey in silence, only now, Lanie realised, the silence was an angry one, fraught with resentment and questions to which there were no answers and for herself, an aching sense of regret. She was relieved when at last they came in sight of the homestead. She didn't even mind jumping in and out of the vehicle to open and close farm gates, she told herself, for anything was preferable to being alone with Jard in his present sardonic mood. Never in her life had she felt so deflated. The sudden plunge from unimagined delight to harsh reality was hard to take. The light shining down on the verandah of the darkened homestead was a welcome sight, and when Jard brought the vehicle to a stop at the foot of the flight of steps she flung open the door and dropped to the ground before he could get out of the Land Rover to help her.

'Thanks for the ride!' she flung over her shoulder as she hurried away. Let him make what he liked out of that! she thought vindictively as she ran up the steps.

'Lanie!' In a few long strides he had caught up with her. 'What's the hurry? You're not trying to avoid me, by any chance,' his laconic drawl was infuriating to her taut nerves, 'because if you are I warn you that you'll never get away with it!' He leaned negligently against the door, effectively barring her way into the house.

'Why would I do that?' she flung at him.

A shrug of broad masculine shoulders. 'You tell me!'

She reached towards the doorknob, but it was useless, for he moved not an inch.

'Relax, Lanie,' his quizzical grin made her wonder what was coming. If he imagined for one moment he could kiss her goodnight ... just let him try! 'About work today——' She realised that a glow on the horizon meant that dawn was very close. She realised another thing, that Jard was back to being the big boss, master of his domain and entitled to give working orders to one of his employees. She wrenched her mind back to the decisive tones. 'Take it easy today, a day off work won't hurt and I'll line up something for you to do tomorrow, right?' He flung open the door.

'Right.' Avoiding his eyes, Lanie hurried inside and sped down the long passage ahead of him. As she ran over the dew-wet grass towards her own domain, a great fan of rose and gold spread over the eastern sky heralding another hot day, but she saw nothing but the entrance to her own room, her sanctuary where at last she could let the tears come unchecked.

CHAPTER NINE

SHE threw herself down on the bed, her cheeks wet with tears as the despairing thoughts chased endlessly through her mind. How could she have imagined even for one moment that Jard's caresses held any meaning, a special message of loving and caring? Oh, she should have known that his real kisses were for Paula. His brief lovemaking to her he would no doubt have already forgotten, regarding it—a shaft of pain pierced her—as nothing more than a boss's privilege.

But to her just his touch could send her world spinning out of orbit, and regardless of the way he felt about her, she longed endlessly to see him, to hear his voice. He was her whole world. How had it happened so swiftly and unexpectedly? she wondered. It seemed that love crept up on you, and it could be too late when you found yourself hopelessly, heartbreakingly in love with a man who was as far out of your reach as any star. Idiot, she chided herself, if you had a grain of sense you would leave here, put yourself beyond reach of his masculine charisma that holds you. But that she knew was something she could not bring herself to do. Not when the days held a promise of being with him and helping him in his work, even if it were only in the capacity of his rouseabout girl!

In the end she must have fallen asleep, for when she awoke, still wearing her crumpled silver-grey dress, the sun was high in the sky. Later, pale and heavy-eyed, she wandered into the living room where Clara was busy clearing away the luncheon dishes.

'I'll leave the food on the table for you,' she offered, but Lanie shook her head. 'A cup of coffee is all I want, thanks.'

'I'll get it for you.' Lanie suspected that Clara's shrewd glance hadn't missed Lanie's lacklustre eyes and

161

swollen lids, but the little woman's voice was bright and cheerful. 'Did you enjoy the dance?'

'Oh yes,' Lanie made an effort to infuse a note of enthusiasm into her voice, 'it was super!'

It could have been an unforgettable night, her heart prompted, it *could* have been!

'I could do with another coffee myself.' Clara was seating herself at the table, her eyes curious. 'You didn't have a row with Mervyn last night, did you? He's been ringing here just about every hour on the hour, but I told him I'd pass on the message for you to ring him back when you came to life!'

'No, no.' Lanie raised her heavy glance. It was difficult to shift her thoughts to Mervyn. 'Everything was fine.'

'That's a relief, because he's certainly determined to get in touch with you.' Clara stirred her cup thoughtfully. 'He must have guessed that Jard would be giving you a holiday today.' Her gaze lifted to a grassy ridge where, in the distance, Jard could be seen riding his white horse Snow, his dogs running alongside, and Lanie followed her glance. 'It doesn't seem to worry the menfolk any, dancing until dawn and then going straight out to work. Jard's on his way to shift some cattle over the far hills.'

'Oh!' Strange, Lanie mused, how empty the day seemed without him.

'Well, look who's here!' Clara was eyeing a dust-smeared car that had come over a rise and was sweeping at speed down the winding track to the homestead. 'Looks like Mervyn got tired of trying to reach you on the telephone and he's doing something about it.'

A few minutes later Clara was bringing Mervyn to the living room, where Lanie still sat at the table. 'He said he wouldn't disturb you,' Clara was saying, 'but I told him you were up and about.'

'Hello, Mervyn.' She forced a smile and hoped he would put her wan appearance down to the all-night dance. 'What are you doing here?'

He grinned and straddled a chair. 'Coming to collect

you—if I can.' Thankfully he took the coffee mug Clara was handing him. 'It's a thirsty drive over the hills! You see, I had this idea——' He had a pleasant voice, Lanie was thinking, slow and quiet, and steady eyes, kind eyes. Not like Jard, who could look at you at times with a message there was no mistaking, speak your name as if the word were a caress and the very next moment spoil it all by saying something hurtful and deflating. She wrenched her mind back to Mervyn's voice. What was he saying? 'So how does that strike you? We could take a run into Wanganui and have a look around, then I'll take you to dinner in town. It might be a change.'

She hesitated. Only a few days since, she would have welcomed the opportunity of spending a day away from the station, especially when the trip would be to a town where she could buy the odd toiletries she was in need of, as well as take in new sights. Now, somehow, nothing seemed to matter very much . . . only Jard.

'Why not make the most of the chance?' Mervyn urged. 'Clara told me you were off the chain today!'

'That's right.' All at once she was remembering something that Jard had said yesterday. He hadn't wanted her to go driving with Mervyn. Indeed, he had been oddly insistent on that point. But what did he really care about what happened to her? And as to telling her what she must and must not do in her free time . . . Bemused, crazy about him as knew herself to be, that still didn't give him the right to order her life, not when he treated her the way he did! 'Right!' Her soft lips firmed and she managed a smile. 'I'd like that. It will be a change to see a new place—should be fun!'

Becoming aware of Clara's puzzled glance, she realised she wasn't making a very good job of acting her part a girl who was happy and carefree. Happily, however, Mervyn appeared to notice nothing amiss. 'That's my girl!' he said on a sigh of relief, and downed his coffee. 'I'll give you ten minutes to pretty yourself up, then we hit the road. Can do?'

'I'll be ready!' She finished her coffee and went to her room. All the time she was sweeping her hair up into a chignon high on her head and changing into pale pink slacks and pink-and-white spotted blouse, her mind wasn't on her appearance. She was too engrossed in anticipating her moment of triumph when Jard would learn that she had taken no notice whatever of his dire warnings concerning Mervyn's standard of driving and had pleased herself about going out with him. Why not, for heaven's sake?

A little later they swept down the winding drive in the direction of the main road and Lanie reflected that even if she weren't all that excited about the visit to the nearest town, Mervyn was looking extraordinarily pleased. He seemed to tune in on her thoughts. 'It's made my day,' he told her laughingly, 'getting you to myself at last! And that's quite a feat!' His sideways glance took in Lanie's profile, the small blunt nose and sweetly curved mouth. 'It takes some arranging, plus a lot of luck!' The car rattled over the cattlestop and they swept at speed around the bends of the driveway, then he braked to a stop at a gate and Lanie got out to open it. When she was once more seated beside him, he flicked her a sideways glance. 'Tell me about yourself, Lanie.'

She said, smiling, 'What do you want to know? My age? Pushing twenty, and don't you dare tell me I look younger! Profession, shorthand-typist. Worked in a city law office for ages then came down here on a cooking stint on a mad impulse——'

'Not all that stuff,' he cut in. 'How about giving me the things that matter—well, they do to me.'

'What sort of things?'

'Can't you guess? Is there a guy back in town who cares a lot about you? I tell myself hopefully that the answer is no. Because if there were he wouldn't let you out of his sight, I know I wouldn't—tell me, Lanie', all at once his tone sharpened, 'is there some man in your life who really matters?'

Lanie felt her heart lurch as on the screen of her mind flashed Jard's strong face. Resolutely she pushed the image aside and forced her voice to a casual note. 'There was, but it was all over between Trevor and me long before I decided to come down to Rangimarie.' An obscure impulse to scotch the cruel rumours that Paula was circulating around the district made her add, 'Trouble was, he just didn't want to believe that I meant what I'd told him about not seeing each other again. That was why he came haring down here after me just after I arrived. Things really got through to him then, at last.'

'Tough on the guy.'

'It would have been a lot harder for him to take if I'd just let things drift on the way they were.'

'Guess you've got a point there—Hey,' his voice lifted on an excited note, 'why am I handing out sympathy to him. I didn't know I could be so lucky!'

They were out on the open road, running alongside a mountain range where bush clung sparsely to high cliffs. Before long they were speeding down into a gully laced with *punga*-ferns to emerge into the hot sunshine on a road cutting through the lush green countryside. At long intervals Lanie caught sight of curving driveways lined with tall poplar trees and leading up to red-roofed farmhouses. Sheep dotted the high slopes and drafting pen were built on the roadside.

Mervyn drove swiftly along the lonely roads, skirting the occasional pile of rubble and earth that had tumbled down from the cliffs above, hugging the earthen banks as they swung around the endless bends. Once she held her breath in alarm as they lurched around a hairpin bend to come on a driver with his dogs, but Mervyn missed a collision with the horseman by inches and ignoring the drover's angrily raised fist, sped on.

At last, through a gap in the hills, Lanie caught the sun-sparkle on water, a passing glimpse of white rolling surf. Beyond the rocky headlands were bleached skeleton trees, the logs piled on the shoreline, then they had left the coastal vistas behind to take a road twisting between slopes covered with the black twisted trunks and umbrella-like fronds of giant tree-ferns. Gradually the remote areas were giving way to small farms, then they were running into Wanganui, crossing a bridge spanning the broad clear waters of a river. 'This is where the jet boat jaunts start up,' Mervyn told her as he braked to a stop close by the bush clad banks of the swiftly-flowing river.

'Care to see anything special, or just tour around?' Mervyn couldn't have been more considerate, Lanie mused. She shook her head. 'I'll leave it to you.' Thank heaven he couldn't guess that today no place held any interest for her, not with Jard so much on her mind. She couldn't seem to banish the image of his tanned lean face, his eyes that could change their expression in a flash. What was Mervyn suggesting now?—she brought her mind back to the present—something about a place name Putiki where there was a memorial church.

So she nodded and smiled. 'I'd like that.' What did it matter to her where they went? she thought dully.

'As tour guide,' he told her a little later as they swept up to a small timber church, 'I suggest you take a look inside.' So she went with him into the quiet building that was so richly decorated with Maori carving and weaving. Then they wandered to the Maori Meeting House nearby with its intricately carved rafters and grotesque figureheads with their gleaming opalescent paua shell eyes. As they emerged from the dim interior of the Meeting House into full sunlight, Lanie blinked her eyes in the sudden strong light. Mervyn who knew the city, took her from place to place. A landscaped waterfowl sanctuary with its illuminated fountains, Kowhai Park on the riverbanks, then they wandered through the beautiful public gardens of the city.

'No wonder this is known as the "garden city".' Lanie was endeavouring to sound animated and happy, but it wasn't easy, for perversely now she was away from the station, she longed to be back there again. Soon it would be dinner time, she reflected. Jard would have come in after his day spent up in the hills. He would have showered and soon he'd be taking his place at the head of the big table. Would he care, she wondered wistfully, that she had defied his orders and had taken off for the afternoon with Mervyn in spite of the warnings?

'Wake up! Wake up!' She realised with a shock that Mervyn was snapping his fingers in front of her face. Heavens, she would have to do better than this or he would end up by guessing her secret. The thought spurred her on to put on her brightest smile and say, 'It really is a lovely town.'

He grinned. 'Only one thing wrong with it that I can see.'

'And that is?'

'The shops are closed today and I can't get you anything to remember it by.' His low tone, the soft expression of his eyes, told her that he really meant what he had said. If only he wasn't the wrong man!

'I don't need anything to remember the trip! Don't worry about it.'

She thought no more of the matter until a little later, as they made their way down one of the main streets in the garden city, he suddenly brought the car to a stop outside a souvenir gift store. 'Who said everything in the town was closed today?' He sent her a triumphant glance. 'You must have something as a souvenir——'

'No, honestly——'

'But you must!' It was clear that he would brook no refusal. Already the girl attendant had come to the open doorway of the store and was eyeing them curiously, and Lanie had no course but to allow him to usher her inside.

'Have you come from overseas?' the attendant asked them in her pleasant way.

'No,' said Mervyn, 'we're just passing through.' He was eyeing the trays of exquisitely set greenstone rings, the jade stones set in gold or silver, the articles made from glittering paua shell with its iridescent shadings of pinks, greens and blues, the woven mats and native carvings and garments fashioned from hand-spun fleeces.

'It's hardly the time of the year for wearing wool,' he whispered to Lanie, 'but it's always a good time for wearing a greenstone ring on your finger——'

Lanie was startled. 'Oh no! They're far too expensive. If you must buy me something, I'd settle for one of those paua shell trinket boxes up on the shelf—they're lovely.'

He didn't spare the boxes a glance, his gaze fixed on Lanie's face. 'You've got such pretty little hands, ever noticed?'

'My hands.' She looked thunderstruck at his words. 'I try to hide them all I can these days. I don't know how I managed to get them in such a mess—well, I do know, but——'

'All the more reason to take up my offer! A greenstone ring will attract all eyes, and no one will ever see the marks of honest toil.'

For a moment she was tempted. Half to herself she murmured, 'If only they weren't so frightfully expensive——'

'Expensive? When there's only one place in the whole of the country where the stone can be found, and that happens to be in such a remote spot that it takes days to get it out and into civilisation. How about this one——' Before she could protest he had slipped the ring on her finger. It fitted perfectly, and it was beautiful, she had to admit. It could have been made especially for her hand.

Mervyn echoed her thoughts. 'It was made for you.' And to the attendant he said, 'I'll take it, please.' Just like that, she mused, before she could protest or argue further.

'Keep it on!' He waved away her thanks. 'It's just something to make you remember the day.' At her hesitant glance, he added briskly, 'Don't worry, no strings, just a gift from an admirer!'

Put like that, she thought, how could she refuse? 'Thank you,' she smiled.

The restaurant to which he took her was a low, attractive place built on the banks of the swiftly flowing river. Wicker tables and chairs were set out on an open-air porch beneath the star-strewn canopy of the soft dark sky and coloured glass lanterns caught reflections in the swirling waters close by. The cuisine was excellent— oyster cocktails, delicately flavoured *toheroa* soup and succulent slices of lamb accompanied by red-skinned tamarillo fruit. Somehow, though, Lanie failed to find any enjoyment in the meal. How could she, when all the time her thoughts were back at the homestead—and Jard. Would he have expected her to return there a long time since? Maybe he would even be feeling concerned at her non-appearance. Stupid! she chided herself. Jard won't even notice your absence.

She wrenched her thoughts back to Mervyn. He was a pleasant and considerate companion, she mused, and he appeared not to notice her lack of appetite and abstracted manner. Maybe he imagined her to be always this way. It was easier to hide her lack of interest, she found when they danced together on the small circle of polished wood in the centre of the scattered tables. Moving to the beat of the melody, she only had to flash on her brightest smile, no matter how she felt deep down inside.

On the long drive back through the darkness she had to admit there had been a certain amount of truth in Jard's warning, for Mervyn drove fast and furiously with no regard for speed limits. His uncle's car was a late-model one with a powerful engine, and a glance towards Mervyn's excited face, told her that he was enjoying the sensation of engine-power and speed, and that for her to caution him in the matter would only serve to make him drive even faster. So she tried not to watch the speedometer needle and braced herself each time they took the blind dark bends at breakneck pace.

She was relieved when they reached the homestead without mishap and he drew up with a scream of brakes at the verandah steps. She felt his lips touch her cheek. 'See you next week!' As she stepped from the car she realised why his farewell kiss had not been a lingering one, for Jard's tall figure was silhouetted in the open doorway.

'Goodbye!' Mervyn called from the window. He

swung the car in the driveway, rattled over the cattlestop and shot away down the drive.

Acutely conscious of the masculine figure waiting at the top of the steps, Lanie deliberately slowed her steps. Maybe, just maybe, she thought with a lift of her spirits, he had been concerned for her safety, just a little.

'Hi, Lanie!' Could it be the shadows thrown by the gleam of the overhanging lantern, she wondered, that made his lean features look more than ever aloof? Well, she would soon change all that! She paused to glance up at him, her glance bright with defiance. 'Miss me?' she enquired cheekily.

'So long as you're okay.' His flat tones gave nothing away.

'Of course I am!' She smiled up into his shadowed face. 'I've had a fantastic time! Mervyn took me for a tour around the town—I'd know my way around Wanganui any old time now—and we finished up with a dinner at a restaurant by the river.'

'Great,' but he looked unimpressed and his tone was dead-pan once again. He hadn't even been listening to her words, she thought angrily.

'I need you to give me a hand tomorrow.'

I need you. She had taken in only the first part of what he was telling her. Crazy of her to imagine even for a moment that he could feel for her the wild attraction against which she struggled without avail. She tried to concentrate on what he was saying. 'I want to shift some cattle that are grazing out on the sandhills. The creeks have dried up over there. We'll catch the low tide and drive them along the beach, it's easier that way.'

'Oh!' She gathered her thoughts together. 'So I guess it's an early start, then?'

'That's the story. See you then.'

'Goodnight.' As she went down the hall Lanie mused that everyone seemed to be in bed. No wonder, it must be very late. For a second the crazy thought shot through her mind that maybe Jard had waited up to

assure himself that she had arrived safely home. Of all
the ridiculous ideas! It hadn't worked out, she reflected
resentfully, her plan of defying his wishes—'orders'
more likely—about driving over the countryside with
Mervyn. Clearly Jard couldn't care less about her. All
that concerned the boss was that she would be here to
shift his cattle at daybreak tomorrow. Once again, she
felt a strong desire to kick something.

CHAPTER TEN

ONE thing about life in the outback, Lanie mused ruefully the following morning, it did accustom you to rising at daybreak. Somehow she didn't even seem to mind. *Not when Jard is waiting for me outside!* The treacherous thought flickered across her mind.

In the empty kitchen she found that he had already breakfasted and gone down to the stables, no doubt to saddle up the horses. So she downed a quick cup of coffee and nibbling a slice of toast, went out into the fragrant early-morning air that echoed with the chorus of birdsong and the lowing of cattle.

When she reached the stables she found Jard throwing a fluffy sheepskin underblanket on the back of a sturdy grey horse. 'Hi,' he greeted her, 'meet Bluey!' Soon he was helping her up into the saddle, then for a moment he stood motionless, an enigmatical expression in his eyes. 'I can always depend on you to be bang on time.'

'Really?' Gathering up the reins, Lanie affected a surprised expression. 'So there is something you approve of about me? You never told me,' she chided him.

He still had that unreadable look in his eyes. 'I've got a lot of things to tell you—one of these days. Meanwhile,' all at once his tone was brisk and impersonal, 'we'll take the track down to the sandhills and shift the steers up to the eastern block. You were cruising around there two days ago. Nothing wrong with the water supply down in the gully, was there?'

To Lanie his businesslike tone was irritating, and definitely a challenge. 'Nothing wrong, boss,' she said demurely, 'creek plenty water, boss!' and before he could make an answer she had dug her heels into Bluey's broad sides and was urging her mount to a

172

faster pace. Soon they were racing over the dried grass as Lanie, leaning low over the saddle, her hair streaming behind her ears in the breeze, guided her mount towards the winding track ahead. She had a start on Jard, but a swift backward glance told her that his white horse Snow had been fast off the mark and was now lessening the distance between the two mounts. It wasn't long before she caught the pounding of a horse's hooves close behind, and almost at once Jard drew level with her. 'Got you!' Catching hold of her bridle, he slowed her to a stop at the top of the rising leading down to the sandhills. She caught his deep exultant chuckle.' You won't get away from me that easily, you know!'

She felt a tingle in her pulses, for there it was again, the deep soft look in his eyes that made her imagine that despite everything he couldn't help liking her—well, maybe even a bit more than liking. 'What makes you think I want to?' But the breeze caught her words and whipped them away, and with an effort she wrenched her mind back to the deep vibrant tones. 'Any idea where we're going?'

She glanced down the slope towards tossing green waves with their white caps, then shook her head. 'Not me, boss, I leave all that to you!'

Presently they reached the sandhills, high mounds of black sand that splintered into a myriad diamond flashes in the sunlight. The wind, blowing endlessly from the sea, sent the fine dark particles swirling around them. Lanie pushed the hair from her eyes and slowed her mount to a walk as the horses plodded over great drifts of sand. When at length they reached the expanse of grass bordering the dunes, she realised the urgency of their trip, for the creek bed held only a trickle of moisture, hoofprints of cattle already baked dry in the muddy surround.

The black steers were scattered over the dried grass edging the sandhills and soon Jard was rounding up the cattle while Lanie turning her mount swiftly, hurried away to block the escape of stragglers and drive them back to join the moving throng. The work, she soon found, was hot and dusty, the crack of Jard's stockwhip cutting across the sound of waves crashing on the cliffs, the barking of dogs and lowing of cattle.

'We'll head them down to the beach!' he called to her. 'Easier to drive them that way!'

Down on the shining sand below the dunes, the tide had receded, leaving pools of water through which the cattle splashed their way along the beach. Lanie soon discovered that the nondescript-looking mount that Jard had chosen for her was a horse who cornered well. Almost, it seemed to her, the sturdy grey anticipated the movements of recalcitrant steers, heading them back over the wet sand in the right direction.

They had left the beach behind and were driving the cattle up the sandy track winding up the slope when she called to Jard, 'You sure picked me a good mount today! Bluey seems to know exactly what I want him to do! He's quick on the turn too!'

He threw her a grin. 'I knew you could handle him. I have to hand it to you, Lanie, when it comes to riding!'

Another attribute in her favour, she mused wryly. Aloud she said lightly, 'I bet you say that to all the young stockmen!'

'Oh, come on, Lanie, you know you're top class!'

A little of the golden lustre of the day faded. Oh, Jard was generous with his compliments when it came to her riding ability, even to handling stock maybe, but when it came right down to the things that really mattered, the man-and-woman things, with him she was definitely a non-starter. He might just as well have been complimenting one of the young shepherds who worked for him on the station.

'What's wrong, Lanie?' His perceptive gaze must have taken in the droop of her soft lips. 'This hasn't been too much for you, has it? This game can be strenuous, especially if you're not used to it.'

She straightened, flinging up her chin. 'I love it! This beats office work any day! It's the work I've always wanted to do.'

The cattle, weary now after the effort of plodding along in the sand, had quietened, and Lanie and Jard were riding side by side, the dogs working to keep the steers moving up the winding slope.

'I could do this for ever!' she exclaimed and saw his face harden.

'So I gathered.'

She said in a puzzled voice, 'What do you mean?'

'Forget it!' he said roughly, and rode away from her and up the rise. What had she said, she wondered, to cause his sudden change of heart? Something about office work? There was simply no understanding him. Her gaze rested on his straight back, his shirt wet with perspiration, the dark blond hair that was catching a patina in the hot sunshine. Jard, Jard, why did you ride away from me? Why do I love you so?

There were no answers to the questions. All at once she was feeling weary. Fine grains of black sand were in her hair and her clothing. She was hot and tired and sticky and sick with a sense of let-down. What had happened to spoil things on this sunshiny morning? She had hoped that riding together, working together, might make him see her, *really* see her. Instead of that . . . She blinked away the silly tears that gathered in her eyes and went on up the track. It was as they turned the next bend that they came in sight of two dust-coated vehicles waiting at the top of the rise.

For a moment Lanie forgot her own problems. 'We've got visitors, by the look of things.'

'Chances are it's a television team,' Jard said. 'They put through a call last month asking me if they could come out here and do some filming. Seems they're putting together a documentary all about back country sheep stations.' He grinned. 'Might just give the townies some idea of what goes on—that is, if they happen to be interested.'

'They seem to be waiting for someone,' Lanie hazarded. 'I wonder what they want?'

'You, actually.' His eyes crinkled with amusement. 'When the crew contacted me they told me I only had to provide one special feature for them and that was a very pretty girl who had the know-how, knew the ropes and how to handle a horse!'

Her heart was behaving strangely, giving a great leap, then steadying again. Jard paying her compliments on her appearance! It just wasn't possible. She sent him a swift enquiring glance, but he was eyeing the two men who had set up their cameras at the top of the slope and seemed oblivious of the earth-shattering remark he had made concerning her. At that moment a steer breaking away from the straggling line of cattle headed wildly up the slope and swiftly Lanie gave chase, her hair, that had long since lost its confining ribbon, streaming out in a cloud of red-gold behind her ears. Not until she had manoeuvred the steer back with the rest did she remember the television cameramen. As she reached the top of the rise, however, a dark-haired young man with a twinkle in his eye stepped forward.

'We've just got some terrific shots of you on your grey. Could you do us a big favour and let us take a few more?'

She realised that Jard had reined in at her side. 'Go on, Lanie. I can handle things now without your help, but I guess these guys can't!'

'But——' All at once she became aware of torn and soiled jeans. In the excitement of cutting off a steer from escape she had ripped her shirt on a bush and the material hung raggedly, exposing a delicately tanned shoulder. Her hair, wet with perspiration, clung in damp ringlets on her flushed forehead and she just knew she had smears of dirt on her face. 'I look awful!' she wailed.

'If you're worried about a bit of sand——' Taking his handkerchief from the pocket of his jeans, Jard leaned over and very gently wiped her sun-warmed cheek.

'I still look a mess!'

'You?' His warm gaze swept her loosened hair and flushed cheeks. He said very low, 'To me you look wonderful.' He was gazing at her, she thought in sudden elation, as if he really meant what he said, and mesmerized by his words, she heard herself saying to the waiting cameramen, 'All right, then.'

'She's all yours!' Jard flashed a grin towards the technicians. 'See you up at the house, Lanie.' A crack of the stockwhip sang through the clear air, then he was riding away in a cloud of dust, leaving Lanie looking bewildered.

'You don't want *me*,' she protested, 'you can't be serious. I only work here, I'm just the rouseabout girl.'

'Whacko!' To her surprise her words evoked an enthusiastic response. 'You're exactly what we happen to be looking for! I'm Tony, by the way,' he had an infectious grin, 'and this sort of slow guy here, he's Stuart. We know you're Lanie, and what we're after is some shots of you on horseback, riding up to the house.'

'I'd say,' Stuart said in his quiet tones, 'that you were definitely photogenic, and with that gorgeous cloud of reddish-gold hair coming out in colour—you don't really object to our taking a few pictures, do you?'

She pulled a wry face. 'It's me I mind, looking such a mess.'

'Don't change a thing! Don't you see,' Tony's voice was laced with enthusiasm, 'that it's something *real* that we're after. Some on-the-spot action shots of a girl who's got looks and riding ability too. You're our honest-to-goodness working girl, remember?'

She smiled in spite of herself. 'How could I forget, looking the way I do?'

Stuart was casting an eye over the surroundings. He eyed Lanie hopefully. 'Reckon you could jump your horse over that log lying over there on the grass?'

'If you like.' Presently she set Bluey to the great fallen *totara* log lying in a paddock not far away, and the cameras clicked as she cleared the low jump. She imagined her ordeal was over, but she soon realised that this was only the start as, again and again, the cameras were trained on her. 'One last shot,' Stuart told her. He was regarding her speculatively. 'I'd like a picture of you taking your grey over that eight-barred sheep fence? How does that strike you?'

'Of course.' Lanie had cleared higher jumps than the barbed fence when taking part in gymkhanas and shows in town, and hadn't Jard told her that Bluey had done well for himself when competing in local showjumping contests?

'Right—you're on camera!' At the signal she set her mount to the barrier and Bluey gathered himself to take the jump, sailing effortlessly over the wire and landing on the other side.

'Tremendous!' The camera team appeared to be delighted with the success of the action shots they had taken, and Lanie bent to pat Bluey's sweat-stained neck. Presently the two men were packing away their gear in the car. 'We'll take a few shots of the track down to the beach,' Tony told her, 'and we'll see you back at the homestead. Don't get out of the saddle, will you, and don't change a thing. We like you just the way you are!'

'That's the trouble. But if you insist——' She rode away to find Jard. When she reached the hill paddock the steers were milling around on the grass and Jard's tall figure was visible among the damp green bush at the foot of the slope. Even before Lanie reached the tree-ferns that clustered in the gully she could hear the sound of water running in the creek nearby.

She reined in at his side. 'Mission completed?'

He swung around to face her. 'My one is. How about yours?'

She smiled. 'Not really. Those television fellows can be very persuasive when they set their minds to anything. They insist on taking more pictures of Bluey and me, and this time the background is to be the homestead steps.'

'What's wrong with that?'

'You sound,' she said, 'simply delighted about the whole affair.' She threw him a teasing glance. 'I expect it's because the documentary they're making will really put Rangimarie on the map, show people what a fantastic place it is. You must be feeling very proud today!'

'I sure am!' There was an odd note in his tone she couldn't fathom. 'But that's not the reason.'

She sent him a puzzled glance, but at something in his eyes she didn't pursue the matter. They turned their mounts and soon they were riding in at the entrance gates to the homestead.

'Help!' Lanie eyed the group gathered at the foot of the verandah steps. 'Everyone's come to watch the proceedings! The word must have been passed along the grapevine and they're all waiting for the camera crew to arrive.' She waved to Mary and Debbie, who waved enthusiastically in return. 'Good for you!' they called. Her gaze moved to Brent, who grinned and sent her a thumbs-up sign, and the two young shepherds smiled shyly in her direction. Edna, still wearing her snowy cooking apron, stood in the front of the group beside Clara, and both looked up at Lanie with approval. At the last moment Mike, the head shepherd, came to join the group.

'I feel such a mess,' Lanie whispered to Jard. 'If only I'd had a chance to clean up a bit and change.'

'You look terrific!' The softness of his tone and his warm appreciative glance sent her discouraging thoughts winging, and excitement pulsed through her veins. What did anything else matter when he was looking at her the way he was at this moment?

'Jard!' Paula came hurrying down the verandah steps looking, Lanie thought wistfully, eye-catching and cool and fresh in her tailored fawn jodhpurs and immaculate cream silk shirt. 'Darling!' She reached his side and gazed meltingly up into his face, the black shining fringe of hair blowing back from her forehead. 'At last you've come back! Honestly, you'd never believe what's been happening around here!' Lanie she completely ignored. 'The TV team are waiting to get some shots around the place. They're making a documentary on sheep stations of the country—and guess what? They want some pictures of a girl who can ride, but I told them they'd have to wait until you got back, then I'd

see about helping them out. Luckily,' she added with
immense self-satisfaction, 'I had my riding gear here.'
She sparkled her bright glance into his eyes. 'Well, what
do you think, Jard? Will I do?'

Before he could answer the question, the camera
team arrived in their car and quickly began setting up
their cameras. Paula turned away. 'I'll have to make
these boys happy!' She approached the two young men,
a dazzling smile curving her lips. 'Here I am, all ready
and waiting! If you want to take me on horseback I'll
get one of the boys to go and saddle up——'

'It's okay,' Stuart cut in smoothly. 'We found a
photogenic subject right on the spot, and everything's
jacked up.'

'What?' As Paula's dark eyes flashed angrily, he
added placatingly, 'Don't worry, we'll get some shots of
you later, just to prove that a girl living in the outback
can show town girls a thing or two when it comes to
looking like a million dollars, tops in hair styling,
fashion garments, make-up, the lot! But for the outdoor
shots, we're looking for the real thing,' he gestured
towards Lanie, 'like Lanie over here.'

'You must be crazy!' Paula's face had turned very
pale. 'I've lived around here all my life,' she spluttered,
'and she's just the rouseabout girl!'

'Thing is, she can ride. Those jumping shots we've
got of her——'

'Ride? I happen to hold the show-jumping championship for the whole of the North Island! Besides,' Paula's
red lips curled contemptuously, 'just look at her! Black
sand and dirt all over her!'

At that moment support arrived from an unexpected
quarter. 'Lanie's your girl!' It was Jard who had settled
the matter. Lanie could scarcely believe what was
happening. The camera team had preferred to photograph her in action rather than Paula, who was really
beautiful, except when she was in a bad humour, as she
was right at this moment. *And Jard had agreed with
their choice.* The wild elation that was surging through
her made her scarcely aware of Stuart's appeasing

tones. 'Look,' he was saying to Paula, 'we've got our girl rider, but we can fit you in with shots of the interior of the homestead. Make you an example of how a woman can be a gracious hostess even though she happens to be miles from civilisation, all that stuff.' He warmed to his subject. 'You could be shown standing beside one of those big Chinese vases up in the hall, and arranging flowers for the dining table. How about that?'

'Thanks very much!' Paula snapped, and turning swiftly, she hurried up the steps. 'Don't trouble yourself about me!' she threw back over her shoulder.

'Pity.' Stuart watched her vanish into the house. He shrugged his shoulders philosophically. 'Oh well, you can't win them all,' he observed to his team mate, 'and so long as we've got Lanie on our side . . .'

The camera crew took a lot of pictures showing Lanie turning in at the entrance on Bluey, approaching the house, seated on her mount at the foot of the steps. Again and again the cameras whirred until at last they sent her a signal. 'Okay, you can relax now. A few shots of the interior of the house and we'll be on our way.' Paula, evidently determined not to make an appearance while the television technicians were working, remained in her room, and it was Jard who escorted the photographers over the weathered old homestead while Lanie rode back to the stables.

She was busy brushing her horse down when Brent came to join her. 'Gee, that's one programme we won't be missing on the TV! How does it feel to be a star?'

Ruefully she eyed her torn blouse. 'Awful! I'm scared to look in a mirror for what I might see! If only they hadn't insisted on taking shots of me as is. I'd love to have got tidied up first.'

He grinned. 'They couldn't risk that. You might have turned up looking a fashion model like Paula. She didn't look too happy about being passed over for you.' Picking up a brush, he too began brushing the sweat and sand from the horse's thick coat. 'Pity,' he muttered, 'that Jard didn't have as much sense as those two guys in the camera crew!'

Lanie pretended not to have caught the candid comment. Until this moment she hadn't realised the interest taken by the staff in the happenings of the station. Somehow it was refreshing and novel to meet someone who didn't belong to the 'isn't-Paula-wonderful' club, even if it was only one of the station hands.

When she got back to the homestead the camera crew had left to spend the night at another station some miles distant, and Paula was seated on a wicker chair on the verandah. No doubt, Lanie mused with a stab of the heart, she was waiting for Jard to return to the homestead.

Paula's glance for Lanie, as she made to pass, was tense. 'Don't let it go to your head! Evidently the TV guys wanted someone ordinary,' the sneering twist to the red lips left no doubt as to Paula's feelings, 'like you!'

Lanie paused, looking down at the lovely, anger-torn face. 'Just what are you getting at?'

Paula shrugged her shoulders. 'You know what I mean.'

All at once across the screen of Lanie's mind flashed a picture of Jard with *that* look in his eyes, his low intimate tone echoed in her mind. *'To me, you look wonderful!'* It couldn't merely be pride that was pricking the other girl, or why did such hatred glow in her eyes? The deprecating feelings that Paula invariably aroused in her fell away and in their place came a newly-found sense of confidence in herself. Paula, who was so utterly lovely to look at—well, when she was in a pleasant mood—and who possessed all the money she required to enhance her beauty, was clearly jealous of *her*! She pondered the matter all the time she took a cool shower, washed her hair under the spray and afterwards changed into fresh panties and bra. Over her towel-dried hair she slipped a cool linen dress in water-lily tonings of palest green and cream, then she went out into the sunshine to drop down on the warm dry grass while the shining reddish-gold strands dried in the breeze.

Lulled by the languorous heat of the day, she was only half aware of voices somewhere close at hand, yet the speakers were out of sight. Probably, she mused dreamily, they were standing on the pathway concealed from her sight by a rose-covered trellis.

'I had to find you, Jard——' Paula's strong carrying tones banished all Lanie's feeling of drowsiness. 'I haven't had a chance yet to tell you why I'm here——'

'First time I knew you had to have a reason for coming.' Jard's voice was tinged with amusement.

'Well, not really, but this time—Look——' There was a note of urgency in the strong feminine tones. 'I've had a message from my friend Anna about Jason and Nita. Anna rang to tell me that the newlyweds are due back from their honeymoon today and Anna's getting up a housewarming party for them tonight. I told her that I hadn't a clue where they're going to live, but she said you'd been to the farm when the other people owned it and you could bring me over there with you and save her the bother of contacting you about the party. You know something?' At the sudden intimacy of Paula's tone, Lanie froze. 'This just could turn out to be the most important decision you ever made in your life, wedding bells and all! I——'

Lanie didn't wait to hear any more. She was running over the grass, scarcely knowing where she was going, only that she must escape Paula's cajoling tones. All the happiness of the day, the companionship of the long ride with Jard over the sandhills, fled her mind and there was only hopelessness and a dreadful ache of anguish. She had known all along that Paula held his heart, everyone knew, so why had she tried to blind herself to reality? The brief occasions when he had seemed to be attracted to her had been no more than her own longing ... and wishing. Paula's words had shown her the utter futility of hopes and dreams, and now even Rangimarie, with its life-style she so much enjoyed, could hold her no longer.

'I'll get in touch with Mervyn in the morning,' she told herself resolutely, 'and tell him that I've changed my mind about that offer of his to take me back to town with him when he leaves here at the end of the week.' At least that will make him happy, she thought desolately, but not me—never me.

That evening at dinner Paula held the conversation that echoed around the table and only Lanie sat silent, Edna's light and fluffy dessert of marshmallow topped with passionfruit lying untouched on the plate beside her. She was scarcely aware of Paula's excited tones as she talked and laughed, effectively silencing any mention of the recent visit of the television crew with a recital of some flattering anecdote concerning herself. Lanie's thoughts were endlessly of Jard and Paula on their long journey through the darkness, together. Had she really managed to persuade herself that by some miracle Jard might come to care for her the way she felt about him? Crazy!

Later, when Paula and Jard were on the way out to the waiting car in the driveway, it seemed to Lanie that Paula, a vivid and arresting figure in her black and silver caftan, appeared more than ever happy and triumphant. Well, why not, prompted her heavy thoughts, when Jard loved her, wanted to marry her?

'Goodbye, everyone!' Paula's brilliant smile hardened as her gaze flickered towards Lanie's sun-warmed face. The next moment she was gay again, blowing kisses of farewell around the room. 'I think they're all jealous of us,' she was clinging to Jard's arm as she gazed provocatively up at him, 'having all the fun tonight!' He said nothing but grinned down into the lovely, laughing face. A few minutes later Lanie caught the sound of a car motor starting up below. If only, she mused despairingly, Paula weren't so utterly lovely. Tonight she seemed radiant, and no wonder! Wouldn't any girl look radiant, *any girl who was loved by Jard!*

In an effort to divert her heavy thoughts she crossed the room and put a record on the stereo, but it was no use, the lilting melody served only to underline her own despairing thoughts. Slowly the evening dragged on, and while the others watched the television screen, Lanie's mind supplied different pictures. Jard would be dancing with Paula. He always danced with Paula, everyone had told her, except of course for the odd duty dance, like giving his rouseabout girl a mercy-spin around the floor on the odd occasion. Edna and Clara, with teasing remarks to Lanie regarding their new television star at the station, went to bed before midnight and only Sandy, who never retired early, stayed to keep her company. If only, she mused bleakly, there weren't the long night hours that bloomed ahead.

At last he got to his feet, stretching lazily. 'Better call it a day, lass, if you want to catch up with your beauty sleep!'

She rose reluctantly. 'I guess.' She was switching off the standard light in a corner of the room when an odd gasping sound startled her and she turned to find that Sandy was slumped back on the settee, his face pallid and a grey tinge around his lips. She had to bend low to catch his muttered words, 'Pills . . . my room.' She was gone in a flash, running along the passage, flinging open the door to his room and switching on the light with trembling fingers. Where would a man keep his life-saving medication? On the bureau—nothing there. The front drawer? The small box was in full view and snatching it up she ran back along the hall. 'Please, *please*, God,' she prayed, 'let me be in time!'

For a dreadful moment, seeing the inert figure, she had a sickening feeling that she was too late, then with shaking fingers she forced the pill through Sandy's colourless lips. 'Sit up, Sandy, try to sit up!' She cradled his head in her arms.

'I'm—okay.' His voice was no more than a whisper.

'What's this?' Jard's terse tones reached her from the doorway, then the next moment he was at her side, his gazing moving from the pills scattered over the floor to Sandy's ghastly features. 'A heart attack? Dad! Wake up! Wake up!'

'It's all right,' Lanie told him on a great sigh of relief.

'I've seen him this way before, and if he gets the pills in time——'

He was scarcely listening to her, she realised the next minute. She had never seen him like this, his eyes dark with shock, his voice stricken. 'You'll be fine, Dad, you'll get over this!'

Sandy's eyelids fluttered and a light of recognition flickered in his eyes. 'Jard! What the hell are you doing back here?' With an effort he raised his head then essayed a weak grin. 'Not to worry. Lanie knows how to look after me.' His low tones strengthened. 'She's had a bit of practice in saving my life. Have to . . . let him into our little secret, eh, Lanie? No use trying to cover up any longer about that other time when I came to grief at the shareholders' meeting in town and you took me home and looked after me.'

Jard was gazing towards her. 'Is that true?' His tone was laced with urgency as if the matter were very important to him. 'Tell me, Lanie, what does he mean?' Before she could answer he had gently drawn her to her feet. 'So that's why he was at your flat in town? That's why he insisted on bringing you down here to work for us? You fooled me, Dad,' the gaze he bent on Sandy was a mixture of love and tenderness and anger all mixed up, Lanie thought. 'And you,' his voice softened and there was a tenderness in it that made her pulses leap, 'you didn't let on——'

'My fault!' Sandy's voice was gaining strength with every moment. 'She was doing it to protect me. I didn't want you to know you had a sick old man on your hands. But so long as I've got medication, and Lanie here, I'll be right as rain! That's why I want her to stay here for as long as she likes. Had ideas,' he managed a wink in his son's direction, 'that things might have worked out that way——'

'Leave that part of it to me!' said Jard. There was a triumphant, excited ring in his voice that Lanie couldn't understand. Unless Paula—Her spirits dropped with a plop, why must she keep forgetting about the other girl?

'I'll be as good as gold now,' Sandy was saying

weakly. 'A good night's sleep and you'll never know
this had happened. I don't need any help, thanks.'
Slowly he got to his feet. 'You stay with Lanie, Jard.
She's the one we have to look after!'

'I intend to. Don't go away, Lanie!' His eyes flashed
a message and there was something in his exultant
glance that sent excitement singing along her veins. As
she watched him helping Sandy out of the room, despite
the older man's protestations, she told herself that she
had no intention of going away just now, not with Jard
speaking to her in that tone of voice, as though he were
promising her something . . . something wonderful. But
of course—she made an effort to wrench her whirling
senses back to sanity—probably he merely wanted to
thank her for being at hand when Sandy was urgently
in need of medication. There she went again, she
scolded herself, dreaming up incredible, heavenly things
all because of a few carelessly spoken words, forgetting
all about ordinary matters like reaction after shock—
and gratitude.

'He'll be all right now.' He was hurrying towards her.
'Lanie——' Suddenly she was trembling, avoiding his
gaze for fear he might glimpse the emotion that showed
in her eyes. He was at her side, taking her small tanned
hand in his, pressing her fingers to his lips. 'I should
have known——'

A shiver of delight went through her. He knew all
about her and Sandy and at last he understood! Then
common sense returned with a rush and she heard
herself saying in a low tone, 'Paula? You didn't bring her
back with you from the party?'

His encircling arm drew her close and his deep
chuckle reached her through a tide of happiness that
was engulfing her senses. 'Don't worry about Paula!
Believe me, it suited her very well to have no transport
back here tonight . . . all part of the project!'

'Project? A wild hope was surging through her.

'Sure!' His encircling arm was drawing her closer.
'Paula's a great girl for the men, but somehow or other
she always seems to get herself involved with the type of

guy she can lead around by the nose. That is, until she fell in love with her own farm manager, and with Mike she met her match! He's not the sort of man she could twist around her finger. They used to fight like mad, then six months ago they finished up with a blazing row and he took off the next day. She put another manager in his place, a married man with a family, but I guess the old magic still holds, and that's why Paula spends so much of her time around here when she could be tripping around the world attending different horse shows. Both she and Mike are as proud as hell and neither will ever make the first move to get together again, but Mike's parents and brothers live not far from here and I guess Paula's always been hoping that she might run into Mike one of these days and put things right between them without losing face!'

'So that was why——' The words escaped Lanie's lips before she could stop them and swiftly she clapped a hand to her mouth.

It was too late. 'Good grief!' His tone was incredulous. 'You didn't get the idea she was hanging around here on my account?'

She threw him an expressive glance from laughing green eyes. 'Well——'

He drew her into his arms. 'Shall I show you how I feel about the only girl in the world I'm interested in?' He bent his head and as his seeking lips found hers she was aware of nothing else in the passionate excitement of his kiss.

A long time later he flicked a finger over her small blunt nose. 'Looks like it's time we got to know each other, sorted things out. Things,' his voice was very soft, 'like my being jealous as hell about you and Sandy. And you,' he grinned, 'getting all het up about nothing at all—Lanie, my little love,' all at once his voice was husky with emotion and his lips on hers sent fire coursing through her veins, 'I've wanted you so. I love you. I can't get along without you. Say you'll stay here with me for ever——'

'I love you too,' she whispered over the joy that was surging through her.

'And you'll marry me?' he urged against her lips.

She threw pretence to the winds. 'Just as soon as you like!'

Then once again his seeking lips found hers, sending her world spinning out of orbit, and she was aware only of his voice, low and infinitely tender. 'I love you, my darling ... love you ...'

Harlequin® Plus

A WORD ABOUT THE AUTHOR

Gloria Bevan has been writing stories ever since she can remember. Painting is her second love, and when writing she sees the scenes of a story in a series of "mind pictures."

Although she was born in a small gold-mining town in Australia, she regards herself as a New Zealander, having come to New Zealand as a small child. She lives in a suburb of Auckland, and through the window of the room in which she writes she can see a vista of sea and the shadowy blue of distant hills.

The mother of three grown daughters, she and her husband, a building inspector, enjoy exploring different areas of the country. Sometimes a story is born in these new surroundings. What else sparks off an idea? "Almost anything can do the trick," Gloria Bevan explains. "It could be a scrap of conversation overheard on a bus that starts the imagination working."

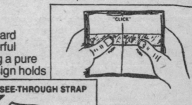

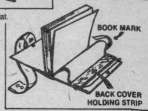